FRAGILE UNION

BOOK 3 IN THE MADE SERIES

BROOKE SUMMERS

SYNOPSIS

Marriages can be fragile, shattered, broken, destroyed...

Holly Gallagher hoped she would find love. That she'd have a happy life, unlike her parents.

Those hopes are dashed when her family arranges for her to marry.

She prays that she won't end up like her mother. Bitter. Twisted. Evil.

That is until she realises who she's marrying. A monster.

Romero Bianchi has given his life to the Famiglia. He doesn't love and he certainly doesn't do attachments.

Everything he's done is for the family. Nothing was going to ever change that.

Until Holly.

She breaks his resolve, piece by piece. She weaves herself deep inside his heart.

He'll do anything for his wife. Protect her with his dying breath.

But being part of the Mafia isn't easy. With enemies at every corner it's hard to know where the threat is coming from.

When Holly's taken, Romero shows the world what happens when someone takes what's his.

Now he's racing against the clock to find her before it's too late.

COPYRIGHT

First Edition published in 2021

Text Copyright © Brooke Summers

All rights reserved. The moral right of the author has been asserted.

Editing by Amy Briggs.

Proofread by Word Bunnies.

No part of this publication may be reproduced, stored in or introduced into a retrieval system, or transmitted, in any form or by any means (electronic, mechanical, photocopying, recording or otherwise), nor be otherwise circulated in any form of binding or cover other than that in which it is published without the prior written permission of the author. Any person who does any unauthorized act in relation to this publication may be liable to criminal prosecution and civil claims for damages.

All characters in this publication are fictitious and any resemblance to real persons, living or dead, is purely coincidental.

BOOKS BY BROOKE:

The Kingpin Series

Forbidden Lust

Dangerous Secrets

Forever Love

The Made Series:

Bloody Union

Unexpected Union

Fragile Union

Shattered Union

Standalones:

Saving Reli

PROLOGUE
ROMERO

I keep my face straight as I watch the beautiful redhead walk into the room. She radiates calm and composure. She's surrounded by deadly men and she acts as though it doesn't affect her. She's either not bothered, or she's good at hiding her fear.

I fight to keep my dick calm as she moves toward her aunt with ease, grace, and sexuality.

Fuck. I want her. I'll have her. In a few months she'll be my wife.

"You must be Romero," Denis says. His accent thicker than his sister's—my sister-in-law—Makenna's, and that woman's is hard to understand at the best of times.

Denis thinks he can intimidate me. His arms are crossed over his chest and his legs spread apart, the scowl on his face is something that'll permanently be there. I'm marrying his daughter and he doesn't like it. Well fuck that, it's business, fucking politics. I don't want to marry Holly, hell no. I'm not the type of guy to settle down and have a family. I'm doing this because I'm getting something out of it. I'm becoming an Underboss. Something I've wanted to be since I was a boy.

"Yes," I reply, meeting his gaze. Nothing and no one intimidates me. If he knew half the shit I've done, he'd be the one cowering right now.

Denis glares at me, and I fight the urge to laugh right now. Fucking hell, this is a farce if there ever was one. I'm marrying a woman I know nothing about so I can become an Underboss. For the Irish Mafia. What the fuck was I thinking? I should have told Makenna no, I could work my way up the pecking order once our father is killed.

"Why don't you three go to my office and talk?" Denis's father, Seamus Gallagher, suggests.

I rise to my feet. May as well get this over and done with. I follow Denis and Holly into Seamus's office and wait.

"Romero, this is Holly," Denis says through gritted teeth as he introduces me to his daughter. My fiancée.

"Hey," she says softly, a timid smile on her face.

Her accent is thick like her father's, but her voice is soft and willowy. My cock jumps to attention. Dammit.

"Holly," I say, rolling her name around my tongue. I let my gaze travel down her body, taking her in. She's beautiful, her hair is red and falls down her back, her cheeks and nose splattered with freckles, her body is hidden behind an oversized sweater and jeans, but I watched her ass as she walked ahead of me. She's got curves and I can't wait to see them.

I'm a lucky bastard, I know that. Holly could have been ugly and I would have been stuck with her, but she's not.

"I know you're becoming an Underboss. I get that you're a made man," Denis begins and Holly lowers her head, her hair falling to cover her face. I scowl at the movement. "But she is my daughter, she's to be protected at all times."

I grit my teeth, I may be a monster, but never to a woman. Ever.

"She gets hurt while she's here, and we're going to have a problem."

I shake my head. "What is it with you Irish?" I ask. "You're too fucking emotional, always wear your heart on your sleeves." Seamus was the same when Dante and Makenna were to marry. They show us their weakness. You don't offer your enemy any information which can be used against you.

Stupid. So fucking stupid.

Denis grins at me. "No one is that fucking stupid," he sneers. "Anyone who'd even go after my daughter would pay with their lives."

I raise a brow. "You threatening me?"

He shakes his head. "The only reason this shit is going ahead is because Makenna assured me you're trustworthy, a man who would protect Holly with your dying breath. My sister is never wrong about people."

Jesus, Makenna has no fucking idea who I am, or what I've done. Not even my brothers know about the depraved things my father had me do—that I still do for him. If it keeps Alessio out of the old man's way, then I'll do whatever the fuck is needed. For my family.

"We done?" I ask, and Holly raises her head, her teeth clamping down on her lip and her gaze darting between her father and me.

Denis's jaw clenches and he nods. I throw Holly a wink as she walks ahead of us and opens the door, a lot more relaxed than when she walked in. Denis on the other hand is pissed off, and I can't help but smirk. I managed to piss him off. Oh fucking well. He shouldn't have tried to intimidate me. That was never going to happen. But the man had better realize that I'd tear his head off if he continues his shit.

When I take a seat, Dante's eyes come to me, the question is clear. Did it go okay? I incline my head ever so slightly and he smiles. My older brother has always been the more composed, the more controlled of the three of us. He is also the one that tows the line with our father more than the rest. That was until he married his wife. I never thought I'd see a grown man lose his damn mind over a woman, but that's exactly what he's done.

I get it. Makenna's fucking awesome. Not only is she the boss, she's also a badass and will kill anyone who even doubts her. It's what Dante needs. I on the other hand don't want the constant back chat and arguments. It's something Holly is going to learn; she is not to disrespect me. I don't give a fuck if she thinks I'm in the wrong, in front of my men and my bosses, she is not to question me.

But at the same time, I don't want a woman that's scared of her own shadow. Her bowing her head while her father and I spoke pissed me off. I have no idea how this union is going to go. I've sold my soul to the devil and in return I've been given a red-headed sexy fiancée. I shouldn't complain, but yet, I feel as though I've been short changed.

HOLLY

THREE WEEKS LATER

HE HATES ME. That's all I can think of when he looks at me. The tightening of his eyes, the clenching of his jaw, and the way he dismisses me whenever I'm in the room while others are there. My fiancé hates me, and yet there's only weeks until the wedding. I don't want to do this but I have no choice. I have to marry Romero.

I've always known I'd be married off; I'd be used as a pawn to secure or strengthen an alliance. It's been drilled into me from a very young age. I'm not like the other women in my family. I'm different and I've always felt less than worthy to have the Gallagher name. Makenna is strong, dominant, she's fierce, protective, and loyal. She's the boss. She's also my aunt, our family is a bit fucked up due to my granda having my da when he was young and then marrying the woman he was promised to. Granda moved to the states when he married the bitch, they had four children and left my da out of their lives.

I grew up without having him in my life, but I didn't miss him. I had my da and my great-granda; I didn't need Seamus. But since I've met him, I've realized just how great he is and I did miss having him in my life. He treats me just as the other men in my life, like I'm weak and need to be coddled.

Then there's Jade, she's my cousin, well sort of. Jade's younger than me, but there's been talk about her becoming an Underboss when the Irish Mafia takes over the Midwest. Jade was kidnapped when she was seven and my aunt lost her mind with worry. Jade's da, Liam, took the very same stance our Uncle Killian did when Makenna had her throat slit. Liam wanted Jade to be able to protect herself, and she can. She's similar to Makenna and everyone loves her.

"Holly," Romero says. I glance up from my laptop and see him standing beside me, his hand resting on the table and his cell beside it. He's staring at me in a way he hasn't before. His eyes heated and his lips thinned. "I'm taking you on a date tonight, be ready at eight."

I blink, what? "Okay," I reply softly, not sure what else I should say. I don't want to go on a date with him; he's made it more than clear I'm not what he wants. "Where are we going?" I ask and his eyes narrow, "just so I know what to wear."

"A dress, we're going to dinner. It's fancy." He grins at me as his phone pings with an incoming text. I'm unable to keep my gaze from straying to the screen of his phone where the text is currently showing.

Georgina: I'm waiting for you, hurry up. I'm horny.

My heart slams against my chest.

"Tonight, at eight," he says and spins on his heel and leaves me staring at the table where his cell was laying.

My heart breaks into a million pieces. I knew he hated me and I knew he didn't want this. But I never thought he'd be with someone else. The tears slowly start to fall and I wipe them away and remember what my ma used to say.

"Men don't define you. They do not own you. You are strong, and you are amazing. Remember that Holly, and never let a man make you feel anything but perfect. Anyone who does isn't worth your effort baby, never give a man more than he can give you."

I'm not sure what happened to my ma, but she used to be a good mam, now, well, now I hate her. But she was right. If Romero wants to screw some other woman. Then let him, I for one will remain a virgin until the day I die. I will not sleep with a man who doesn't respect me enough to be faithful.

Once the tears are finally dried, I get back to work, trying to keep my mind off what Romero's doing with a woman named Georgina.

Welp, at least I know this marriage isn't going to be anything like Dante and Makenna's.

ONE
ROMERO

TWO MONTHS LATER

"You know that Kenna wants to rip your balls off," Dante tells me with a smile. He's a twisted son-of-a-bitch, he loves when Makenna brings out her crazy side. The more bloodshed the better for the two of them.

I glance around the room, wondering where the hell Alessio is with the damn bottle of whiskey. I need a damn drink. He disappeared almost twenty minutes ago in search of a bottle. I thought he'd have been back by now.

"Why, what have I done?" I ask, wondering if she's just extra temperamental now she's pregnant.

"Something about a woman that's here," he says. "Holly is pissed."

I frown, "Why is she pissed? What's happened?"

He shakes his head. "You really can't be that fucking stupid," he clips out. "Why the fuck is Georgina here? I mean, do you have a death wish? Fuck, does she have one?"

Now that's a question I want answers to. I want to know why that bitch is here. She wasn't invited. I made it perfectly clear months ago she was to steer clear from me and my soon-to-be-wife.

"How did Holly find out about her? I thought you ended things with her before Holly came to live with us?"

My gut clenches as I remember the pain that slashed through Holly's face when she saw the text Georgina sent me.

Georgina knew as soon as I agreed to marry Holly our arrangement was over. She knew nothing would ever come from it. She was convenient and there. Easy. I don't work hard for my women, I never have. Georgina runs in our circle, she's in the life, and her uncle is head of the Carter Syndicate. She knows to keep her mouth shut, it's the only reason I kept her around longer than a month.

I've never been one to give a fuck about what people think, but knowing my soon to be wife was hurting when she saw the message from Georgina fucking broke something inside of me. Since that day, I've tried to get closer to her, show her I'm not that much of an asshole, but it seems whenever I make progress I end up pissing her off and she'll glare at me.

"Are you listening to me?" Dante demands and I sigh. "Don't fuck this up," he growls, "you hurt Holly and there's nothing I can do to save your fucking ass. Don't you understand that?"

Anger spears through me. When did he become this bastard?

I stare at my brother in disgust. "What happened to you? Hmm? Where's the man who would rip anyone's head off if they even thought about threatening your family?"

He steps closer to me, his nostrils flaring as his jaw

clenches. "You're going to be an Underboss now, Romero. It's time to be accountable for your actions."

I shake my head. "Ice," I scoff, using his nickname. "You're not even there. You're letting your wife lead you around by the balls. Grow a fucking pair, Dante."

He moves quickly so we're face to face, his forehead pressing against mine. He's got a few inches on me in height but I have more muscle. "You are my brother," he snarls at me. "Don't you dare fucking disrespect me. I have your back, I always have. But you fuck up with Holly and you're putting me in the position to choose between my wife, who is the mother of my fucking child, and you. That will piss me the fuck off."

I don't say anything and I don't back down. Fuck that, I'll stand my ground until the day I die. It's the way I was raised. Never back down, don't give someone the upper hand.

"You always were a fucking little shit," he gripes as he takes a step backward. "I'm not going to war if you can't keep your fucking cock in your pants."

I glare at him. "If you must know, I told that fucking bitch to stay the fuck away from me before Holly even arrived in the states. Georgina obviously hasn't gotten the message yet, but don't worry, brother," I say through clenched teeth, "you can reassure your wife I won't hurt precious Holly."

He narrows his eyes at me. "Just to let you know, brother," he fires back, "Holly never told Kenna why she's upset. It was Alessio who let the little bomb of Georgina showing up drop. Holly hasn't mentioned you at all to Kenna, and that's why my wife is suspicious."

Fuck, I thought for sure she'd have told her aunt about the text message she saw, but she hasn't.

The door opens and Alessio pushes through. "Over two hundred people at this wedding, the majority of them Irish, why the hell is there no fucking alcohol?"

"Because if there was alcohol before the wedding, we'd have a fucking drunken mess on our hands," Makenna says as she strolls into the room. "Would you mind giving Romero and I a moment alone?"

Alessio immediately slips out of the room and Dante glares at me before following behind him. I stand here and wait for her to begin her threats of what will happen if I hurt her niece.

"I think you and Holly need to talk," she begins and I raise a brow. "This tiptoeing around each other shit has got to stop. You're going to be married, and while I'm a bitch and will come out and tell you that you're an asshole if you've pissed me off, Holly won't. She buries it, let's it fester, and she grows distant."

I cross my arms over my chest and tilt my head, studying her. I don't get it, why is she here, talking about this? "Why are you telling me this?"

She sighs. "I like you, Romero, I really do. I think you're a good man and you'll be perfect for our Holly when she gets over whatever the fuck happened. You'll protect her unlike anyone but her father can, you'll love her like no one else, and you'll cherish her like she deserves."

I hold back the scoff. Love? Really?

"Holly takes things to heart. Way more than she should and I can't blame her. That bitch of a mother of hers needs to be shot for the way she treats Holly. So, my niece is closed off and tries to protect herself by keeping her guard up. Fix whatever the hell happened, and then be her husband, Romero."

"Makenna, where the hell did you get this idea that I'm

going to be this fucking perfect husband? I don't do love. I don't even want a fucking wife."

"I know, but have you considered what this means for you?" she says.

I frown, what the fuck is she talking about?

"Holly is untouched, Romero, she's going to be yours. Yours to protect, yours to cherish, yours to love. Only yours."

Her words are like a punch to my gut.

"You need to stay out of my fucking head." I scowl at her. She's the only one who seems to get inside of me and see past the darkness.

She grins at me. "Think about what I said, you've never had that before. But you also have to realize that neither has Holly, she's never had anyone that's all hers."

"What?" I hiss. What the fuck does that even mean?

She shakes her head. "That's for Holly to tell you when the time is right."

The door opens and I fully expect it to be Dante ready to reclaim his wife, but instead I see Georgina. Her brown hair cut shorter than usual, stopping under her chin. The dress she's wearing is a pale cream, almost on the verge of white, it's strapless and hits her mid-thigh. Her lips are twisted into a scowl as she glares at Makenna.

"Isn't it bad luck to see the bride before the wedding?" Georgina sneers as she steps toward me.

Makenna gives her a shark's grin. "Oh, hon, I am not his bride and you do not want to tangle with me."

Now that's something I'd fucking pay money to see. Makenna kicking her fucking ass.

"What the fuck are you doing here, Georgina?" I bite out, wondering why she's even in my room, or how she knew where I'd be.

She runs her finger over the buttons on my shirt. "I

wanted to see you," she breathes, as she pushes up against me. "I thought you might want to have one last fuck before you marry the ugly bitch."

My hand wraps around her neck. "That's my fucking wife you're talking about," I snap. I've had enough of this fucking cunt. "I told you months ago I wouldn't be going anywhere near your ass again. You reek of desperation. What did you think would happen, that you'd text me thinking I'd run to you?"

Her face is red and her eyes are wide. "Romero, please, we were so good together."

I shake my head as my fingers tighten around her neck. "No, fuck no. You do not act as though we were more than we were. You have a great mouth, that's all you have going for you."

Tears fall down her cheeks as she grips my hand. "Please," she begs.

I release her and take a step back. My gaze goes around the room and I see Makenna's not the only one in the room with me. Holly, Dante, Alessio, and Denis are all here too. Holly's eyes are wide but the guys are all smug as fuck.

"This is the last time I tell your ass, Georgina, contact me again and you'll not like the result. Fuck with my wife and I'll end you."

She huffs as she rushes out of the room, not before glaring at both Makenna and Holly. She even thinks of doing anything to my wife, I'll make sure she'll regret it. I'll go after everyone she holds close.

"Seems as though Kenna was right," Denis says into the silence.

I turn to him. "About what?"

He grins. "Holly, don't be long," he tells her as he places

a kiss on her head before he, Dante, Alessio, and Makenna leave the room.

I finally take her in, and as always something in me stirs. I'm not gone like Dante was over Makenna, that fucker practically fell in love at first sight. But I do have some protective instincts toward her. To say I'm attracted to her is an understatement. The woman is fucking gorgeous and funny as hell. She's quick-witted and always has a comeback, albeit they're usually aimed at me as I've pissed her off. She's wearing sweats, her hair is in curls at the top of her head, and she's not wearing any makeup. Yet, she's still one of the most beautiful women I've ever laid eyes on.

"So," she begins, her voice soft, it's something I've learned about her. She never raises her voice. Ever. "You didn't go to her that day? I know you knew I saw the message." Her Irish accent soft, sometimes I have to strain to understand her, thankfully, now isn't one of those times.

"Yeah I know, I'm not blind. I also thought you'd have the courage to ask me outright."

She narrows her eyes at me. "You're an arsehole most of the time, Romero, why would I think you wouldn't have gone to her? The message made it seem as though you messaged her first." Her lips curl in disgust.

I take a step toward her like a predator inching toward its prey, and smirk when she holds her head up high. "I'm a fucking asshole, Holly. I'm never going to change. I'm a depraved monster who has no qualms in slaughtering families. I'll happily do so with a goddamn smile on my face. You are going to be my wife. It's time for you to start acting like it."

She tilts her head to the side and studies me and I realize she's more like Makenna than I realized. "What do you want me to do?"

"Act like the princess you are. Don't let anyone fucking try and take what's yours. I can guarantee no one will be taking what's mine."

She raises her perfectly shaped brow, a smile tugging at her lips. "I'm not yours, yet."

Oh she's just fucking poked the bear. Possessiveness rears its motherfucking head, and I slam my lips against hers, as my hands fly to her waist and I pull her against me. I'm loving that she whimpers as I push my tongue past her lips and possess her mouth, dominating it; her moans are more than enough encouragement.

I'm rock fucking hard and so close to pushing her against the wall and fucking her.

"You're mine, Holly," I grunt when I pull back.

Her lips are swollen and pink, her cheeks red from the heat, and her eyes are wide with lust. She looks fucking perfect, and I can't wait until I finally make her mine.

Makenna was right, having Holly, who's untouched, will make me possessive of her. All of the women I've been with have been with either one of my brothers and while I don't usually mind, I know I'd kill them if they ever thought about trying that with Holly.

"Fine," she huffs. "But make no mistake Romero, you cheat on me and I'm going for your balls."

I smirk at the angry threat. God, she's fucking beautiful when riled up.

She narrows her eyes on me. "Why the fuck do you think that's amusing?"

"Chill, baby, yeah? Today's going to be a good day."

"If you say so, Ma's a fucking nightmare." She sighs as she rubs her chest. "Do what everyone else does, ignore her. She craves the attention. Just don't give it to her."

"What's wrong with your mom? Makenna said she was a

bitch." I remember she also said she just had a baby. Holly's twenty and she has two older brothers along with younger siblings.

She glances at the door before her gaze swings back to me. "Ma is a bitch, Romero. She hates her life so she has to make everyone else's life miserable. Da despises her. I don't think he ever liked her; he's never loved her. But she hasn't helped matters, she's been fucking around on him since before they got married."

I manage to keep the shock off my face. Fucking hell, why is the bitch still alive?

"Da realized when she was pregnant with Chloe, he knew she wasn't his daughter." She shudders. Her voice willowy, her Irish accent always a little thicker when she speaks about her mom. "I have no idea why Da keeps her around, all they ever do is argue, and then she fell pregnant with Mary who's almost a year, and I knew Da was done, but of course, Ma got pregnant again, and Gareth was born last week. You'd think she'd have some sense, I mean, she has to know her husband will kill her, but she doesn't care."

Fuck.

"I don't have to tell you, I'm nothing like your father, but Holly, you even glance at another man and you'll regret it."

She narrows her eyes. "Sleep with one eye open arsehole."

I chuckle. "I mean it, I don't share, not you, not ever. Even try it and I'll kill you."

She rolls her eyes and pats my chest like I'm a child. When the hell did she lose her fucking shyness around me? "Sure, whatever you say, big guy. We both know I would never do that, but I should inform you, Danny has taught me how to use a knife and if you cheat on me, you'll lose your balls."

She kisses my cheek and moves toward the door. "Please try not to be late. I'm going to need alcohol around my ma, and the sooner the wedding ceremony is over, the quicker I get a drink."

"You Irish have a serious problem."

She shakes her head, not in the slightest offended. "Nah, we don't. We're able to handle our drinks. You're considered a light weight if you get drunk after a few drinks." She grins widely at me. "We'll see how well you hold up."

"Go, baby, I'll see you soon."

"I'm not your baby, Romero," she bites, but she eases the sting by blowing me a kiss as she leaves the room.

"Sooooo," Alessio begins as they walk back into the room, "that went a lot better than I thought it would have."

"What's that supposed to mean?"

"Okay," Makenna says clapping her hands. "I love you guys, but you need to start getting ready, you've got less than an hour before the ceremony begins. Which also means, I've got to start getting dressed too."

"He's fine," Dante assures her. "Go, we're fine."

I turn my back on them and reach for my jacket. Once I hear the door close, I ask Alessio again, "So?"

"Rome," he shakes his head, "we all know Makenna's a badass, but Holly, if looks could kill, we'd all be dead. It's true what they say, redheads have a fiery temper."

He's trying to piss me off. "Whatever." I shrug on my jacket, wishing he'd found some whiskey somewhere, I could use a shot or two.

He holds his hands up. "I like her, that's all."

My head snaps up and I pin him with a glare. "What?"

His eyes widen and I see the grin on Dante's face. "Relax, Rome, he's not going to poach. She's all yours."

Dante tries to assure me but the fucking grin he has isn't helping matters.

Alessio runs his hand through his hair. "Fuck, you were right. What the hell is it with these Irish women? They make you all go fucking crazy."

Dante slaps him on the back. "Come on, let's go before he punches you. I can't wait for you to find your woman. She's going to knock you on your ass."

I finish getting ready and can't help but wonder what the fuck is going on? Why am I so protective of Holly? I barely know her. Whatever happens, I'll not go down like Dante. He's lost his damn mind where Makenna's concerned.

TWO
HOLLY

"Da, please, keep her away from me," I plead with him. Ma's already started her shit today and I don't want to listen to it anymore.

"She'll be on her best behavior, I promise, baby girl." He pulls me into his arms and I go willingly. I'm such a daddy's girl. My da loves me and he's not afraid to show it; he's the best da in the world. When Ma was off doing God knows what, or God knows who, Da was the one who would read me stories, he'd be the one who never missed a recital, or a meeting with the school.

He gives a fuck about us kids and that's why he's the best man I know.

"Why is she even here?" Malcom asks, his teeth clenched and his eyes filled with pain.

Something's happened with him, I'm not sure what, but I do know that he's changed in the past few months, ever since we found out Melissa was pregnant. I adore my sister-in-law, she gives my Aunt Makenna a run for her money in the badarse stakes. I'm worried about Mal, he's always been the quieter of us, always watching rather than engaging, but lately he's withdrawn and I hate it.

"She's your ma, you know what she's like," Da says and I roll my eyes. "I've warned her, she's wearing on my last nerve."

"You should have put her down a long time ago," Mal growls as he watches her saunter into the room. "She's got some fucking nerve."

"Malcolm." She smiles at him as she walks over to us. When she reaches my brother she goes to kiss his cheek but he snarls at her and walks off. "Well, that wasn't polite."

"What did you do to him?" I ask. "He's always been the only one of us who gave a fuck about you ma, so what did you do?"

She glances away unable to meet my gaze and that's when you know she's done something wrong. "One day, couldn't you just be a human for one bloody day?" I cry.

She narrows her eyes at me. "Don't you dare talk to me like that, are you fucking forgetting who raised you?"

I scoff, "Ma, you gave birth to me, you didn't raise me. You haven't raised any of your children. And you certainly aren't going to raise Gareth, I mean he's only a week old and you've already left him," I bite out, having had enough of her.

"Holly, remember your respect," she hisses. She glances down at me, I'm in my robe, my hair and makeup are done, and I'm waiting to put my dress on. "God, you could have lost some weight before you got married."

"Out," Da snarls, his hand clamping around her wrist. "You're done. I fucking warned you, bitch." I watch with watery eyes as Da practically drags her out of the room.

"Don't cry, Hols," Malcolm whispers as he comes back into my room. "She's not worth your tears, princess."

I shrug. "I should be used to this by now, she hates me, she always has." It shouldn't hurt anymore, but it does. It stings deep and I'm angry at myself for letting her affect me.

"She's deflecting her shite onto everyone else, Hols. She's jealous and you're not fat, far fucking from it. When you marry Romero, get him to feed you, yeah?"

I giggle at his words, he's always had this thing about feeding me. He used to cook me pancakes every Sunday while Da had a meeting with all his men. Malcolm would ensure I was fed before he left to join them.

"Mal, talk to me, what's happened?" I whisper, afraid he'll walk away and not answer but at the same time, scared he will answer and whatever it is will break my heart.

"You know how Mary, Chloe, and Gareth aren't Da's?"

I nod. We all know, and we've tried to keep it under wraps, not wanting the men to find out Ma's an adulterer.

"Well, they're not the only ones."

I suck in a sharp breath. "No." The tears once again springing to my eyes.

His eyes are wide and he swallows hard. "Yeah, princess, Ma's a fucking bitch and Da ain't my Da."

I shake my head. "He is your Da, Mal, he'll always be your Da. Don't you ever say that to him, he'll be heartbroken."

"I know," he whispers as he pulls me into his arms. "I don't know if she ever told him, or not."

"It doesn't matter, you're his son," I insist, knowing Da, if he finds out he's going to kill Ma. I'm in shock, I can't believe it. "How did you find out?"

"Ma was in a rage after Danny boy's wedding, she was pissed and decided some truths were to be had."

My heart sinks, why is she so evil? "I'm so sorry," I whisper as I rest my head against his shoulder. "You know this doesn't change anything right? You're still my brother and I love you dearly."

"Love you too, Hols," is his gruff response. "Come on, let's get you ready so you can get married. Where's Makenna?"

"She'll be here in a minute, she's bossing everyone around."

He chuckles. "Sounds about right. Thanks, Hol, I'm sorry for being an arse and dropping this shit on you."

"Don't be. Ma did this, not you."

There's a knock at the door and we both glance to see Da walking in. "Come on, kiddo, it's almost time to go."

Mal drops a kiss on my cheek. "I'll see you in there."

"You ready, baby girl?" Da asks once we're alone.

"Yeah," I whisper as my nerves start to hit me.

"He's a good man, Holly. Makenna would never have agreed to it if he weren't."

I nod because I know he's a good man. I also sense there's a darkness swirling inside of him. He's so intimidating, it takes everything in me not to squirm under his gaze.

"Get your dress on, and then we'll get you married."

I suck in a deep breath and smile. "Okay, Da."

"YOU LOOK BEAUTIFUL, BABE," Romero whispers quietly as we're greeting our guests.

The wedding went off without a hitch, and thankfully, it's so much different to the way Makenna's and Dante's ended.

"Babe?" I ask while trying to hide my smile.

He grins, knowing that I'm fucking with him. "It's either babe, baby, or doll face."

I blink. "Doll face?"

His grin widens. "Your skin is so fucking pale and soft it reminds me of those fine china dolls my mom used to have."

Butterflies swarm my stomach at his words.

"Yeah, doll face it is." He leans forward and places a hard, chaste kiss against my lips. "I know things are going to be weird for us," he says as he pulls me close to him ignoring the people who want to wish us well. Thankfully, Da, Danny, Makenna, and Dante greet them for us. "The way things started with Georgina and her crap, but you're my wife now, Holly."

"Do you want a marriage like Makenna and Dante?" I try and keep the hope out of my words.

He sighs. "I'm not capable of love. I can promise you that I'll care for you, but I doubt I'll ever love you. It's not who I am."

I lick my lips as the pain slashes through me. "So, what is it that you want?"

His eyes blaze with lust. "I want you, we're married, and that means something to me. I am not my father and I'm not your mother. We took vows, ones we're going to live by."

I stare into his beautiful brown eyes. "I can do that," I promise him. "I'll be your wife, Romero."

"Rome," he tells me. "My brother's call me Rome, and you can too."

I sink further into his embrace. "Rome," I repeat and can't help but think that maybe, just maybe I've made a little headway with my rugged made man.

"Well, well don't you two look cozy," the sneer is loud enough for us to hear.

My lips snap shut, and I grit my teeth as my body bristles. Jesus, Mary, and Joseph. Fucking Georgina.

"Doll face," Rome says so only I can hear him, "when a

bitch, any bitch, threatens what we have, what we're growing, you don't back down. You stake your fucking claim and make it known. You are mine and I am yours."

I stand up taller and face her. He's right, he is mine and I'm his. He's also the Underboss and he deserves respect. I am his wife, the daughter of the head of the Irish Mafia and the Great-granddaughter of the original leader of the Clann. I deserve the respect.

"And don't you look desperate," I say with a bright smile on my face. "I mean, you've already been told nobody wants your skanky arse, and yet you're still here."

Her cheeks pink as she stamps her foot. "You little..."

I shake my head. "Ah, ah, ah. Now we learn this shit when we're at school. You do not throw a tantrum when you don't get your own way. Now stop being a desperate slag and please feel free to go to the bar and get yourself a drink. I'm sure as the night wears on, the alcohol starts to flow, and the beer goggles start to come round, you'll be able to persuade some poor unassuming fella to bring you home."

Romero's hand tightens on my hip. "You were warned, Georgina." His voice filled with anger and she shudders. "I fucking told you what would happen if you came after my wife."

She narrows her eyes at us. "Why?" she asks. "Why her? What does she have that I don't?"

I suddenly realize why she's so desperate. She's lost the man she loves.

"So fucking much," he tells her, his tone getting colder by the second.

"Now, you've been told to move on," Da says, injecting himself into the conversation. "You have a choice," he says with a wicked smile. "You can go to the bar and get a drink.

Fuck. As many as you want, it's an open bar. But you stay, you leave my son and daughter alone."

"Or," Makenna says, stepping up to her so they're face to face. "You can carry on being a fucking bitch and I'll have no problem laying you out. I don't give a fuck if that means going to war with your uncle."

"Georgina." The heavy sigh of a man pushing through the throngs of people has Romero on edge, and his hand at my hip tightens even more. "What the fuck do you think you're doing?" He grips her wrist and pulls her roughly to him. "I apologize for my niece," he says to Romero, Makenna, and Dante. "We'll be on our way."

"Like I said," I begin and I see my Da smirk. "If she can behave herself, she can stay. She's only upsetting herself. She doesn't matter to us."

"Atta girl, doll face," Romero praises me.

"Carter, sort her out," Da grounds out and it's weird to see this side to him. Around us he's easy going and fun loving. But then he can switch so quickly. It's clear to see why he's the boss.

"Mr. Carter, please have a wonderful evening and thank you for joining us in celebrating our union," I tell him with a bright smile.

He's caught off guard; from the way Da and Romero are scowling at him, he didn't expect to have me be nice.

"Thank you, Mrs. Bianchi," he says with a smile. "You're a lucky man, Romero. Congratulations."

"Fucking asshole," Romero grunts when Mr. Carter leaves. "Doll face, can I just say, that was fucking epic. I mean, I know you were pissed but you kept your cool and killed them with kindness."

"That's our Holly," Da says as he kisses my cheek. "Don't let that tramp get you down."

"Romero was right. You're so much fucking better than that bitch, she was so desperate for attention she practically wore white to your wedding."

"Come on, let's get you some food, you've not eaten since breakfast," Romero says as he begins to lead me away from the throng of people.

Malcolm catches my eyes and smiles. For those words alone I know Malcolm approves.

"Holly, did you really have to wear that?" Ma sneers at me hours later. God, I forgot she was here. Somehow, she had managed to keep her mouth shut for a few hours and kept away from me.

Georgina and Mr. Carter left a while ago, only staying for an hour before he dragged her out of here. I thought the drama and bullshit had left but I was wrong.

I watch in shock as Melissa reaches for Ma's arm. "That's enough, Zoe," she says as she pulls her from the reception room.

I go to stand, but Romero puts his hand on my shoulder stopping me. "Leave her, doll face. She's a fucking cunt and if she says one more derogatory thing about you, I'll forget she's a woman and fucking end her."

"He's right, Hols, leave her. She's obviously been pissing the women off today. What happens, happens, she deserves it," Mal says cryptically and now I'm wondering if something is going to happen other than them talking.

My eyes glance at the door they've just gone through and see both Da and Danny follow the girls out. God, Melissa doesn't need this stress, she's pregnant.

I'm anxious as I wait for them to return, every time there's movement by the door, I turn to see if it's them. Finally, Makenna strolls in with a smile on her face, "Your ma's gone to bed, she won't be down for the rest of the evening. So, sit back, relax, and enjoy the rest of the reception," she tells me.

Mal laughs. "What did you do to her?"

She shakes her head. "Nothing, I didn't get a chance."

I raise a brow. "Huh?"

Romero throws his arm around my shoulders and pulls me into his body. "Denis beat you to it?" he asks her.

"Not him..." she says, but turns her attention to the door. I follow her gaze just in time to see Danny smack Melissa's arse. The two of them oblivious to the fact that everyone's staring at them. They're so caught up in each other. They're in love. It's something I've always wanted. The all-consuming love that'll bring you to your knees. It wasn't something I grew up around, didn't know if it truly existed. But it was what I craved. Now, I know I'll never get it. That I'll never have the love that my brother feels for his wife. Deep down it hurts. It fucking stings. But I'm married now and there's nothing I can do about it.

"Well if it wasn't Da, who did and what did they do?" Mal asks, pulling my attention from Danny and Melissa.

"She did." Makenna points at Melissa. "Your ma pushed us too far today and Melissa snapped. She has a dislocated shoulder, a broken nose, a busted lip, and she was unconscious."

"Fucking hell," Romero mutters. "Are all the women psychos?"

"Yep," Mal says with a smile, "even our Holly has her moments."

I narrow my eyes at him. "No, I don't."

He grins. "You fucking do. You're more twisted than the rest of them. It's why you and Jade get along so fucking well," he says talking about our cousin. I haven't seen her in a while, she lives in Chicago with my auntie, uncle, and cousins.

I raise my head and glare at him. "I resent that."

Makenna throws her head back and laughs. "It wasn't you who signed Alessio up to the male porn monthly subscription?"

I bite my lip. Yeah, that was me.

"Or," she continues, "it wasn't you who gave Killian's number out to the priest?"

I close my eyes as Romero's body starts to shake beside me.

"He still calls him now, trying to get him to see the right path." Makenna continues.

"And wasn't it you who added hair removal cream into Alessio's shower gel?" Dante asks with a smile.

"You told me it was a faulty batch," Alessio fumes his eyes wide as he stares at me. "Those fucking magazines are still coming. You need to get rid of them."

I smile sweetly at him. "I have no idea what you're talking about."

Dante snaps his fingers. "It was you, wasn't it?"

I tilt my head. "What was me?"

"You're the one who changed all Rome's passcodes." He throws his head back and laughs. "Oh, I fucking knew it would be fun having you around. I just didn't know how much fun it would be."

Ah yeah, that was me. He shouldn't have pissed me off.

"Make sure you keep me out of your games," Dante demands.

"Don't piss us off and you'll be fine," Kenna assures him and of course it has the two of them bickering.

I turn to face Romero who's been quiet since he found

out I changed his passcodes. He's got a smirk on his face and relief washes through me. "So, you have a vengeful streak?"

"The worst," Danny says as he and Melissa come to sit down at the table. When I face him, I see he has his arm thrown around Melissa's shoulder, like Romero's is around mine. "One time, she found out I was the one who told Da that she sneaked out of the house and she got grounded. She put laxatives in my coffee, fake tan in my shower gel, and she took all the petrol from my car."

Mal chuckles as he was the one who helped me with siphoning the petrol from the car.

"She's a sadistic bitch. Her best motto is, 'revenge is a dish best served cold.' I swear you could have pissed her off months ago and you'll think she'd forgotten it, until you wake up with wax strips attached to your body," Danny says with a rueful smile.

"You're so fucked, Rome." Alessio chuckles.

"Oh, that's not even the worst she's done," Makenna announces. "She saves the best stuff for her ma. I mean putting green dye in Zoe's shampoo was probably the best day of my life. I'll never forget that bitch's outrage."

"Ma still has no idea it was Holly," Mal says as Da joins us, he's already got a pint of Guinness in his hands and looks pissed.

"Doll face," Romero says softly and I turn to him once again. "No matter how much I piss you off, don't do that shit to me."

I smile at him. "Sure, whatever you say, hon."

If he pisses me off, he's going to know about it. As my da says, kill him with kindness and if all else fails, then fuck with them so they'll think twice about making the same mistake again.

THREE
HOLLY

"This has been a great reception," Da says, "I'm sorry about your ma, I didn't think she was that stupid, baby girl."

I shrug. "It's grand, Da, it's not your fault." Well, it kind of is, he should have ended their marriage a long time ago, but he hasn't and I'm not sure why. "Are you okay?"

He flashes me a smile. "I'm fine. Are you happy?"

God, that's a loaded question, one I can't answer truthfully, so I lie. "Yeah, Da, I'm happy."

It's not fully a lie. I'm happy I get along with Rome, I'm happy I get to be around family, and I didn't have to move to a new city without having Makenna. But I'm not happy that my new husband will never love me.

I'm jolted forward slightly as a hand rests at my back. I immediately know from the heat that spreads throughout my body that it's Romero. "Doll face, are you ready?"

My body screams no I'm not, but I mutely nod.

"Goodnight, Holly," Da says kissing my cheek, "we'll see you both in the morning before we fly back."

My heart hurts, not only will he be leaving, but so will Malcolm, Danny, and Melissa.

"Night, Da." I give him my best bright smile, the one no one has realized is fake.

It took me years to perfect. I guess that's something I've learnt of my ma, and she's great at faking shit. Her marriage, her love, and her life.

Rome takes my hand and leads me away from the last of the lingering family. Most have gone to bed, it's almost two in the morning.

"There's no need to be tense," he tells me as we step into the lift. "I'm not going to maul you as soon as we get into the room, I have a little more finesse than that."

His words make me feel less nervous, but I still can't relax. The unknown is making it worse. I glance at him. "You? Finesse?"

His lips twitch. "I've learned a lot about you tonight, doll face."

"And yet, you don't know the half of it." We don't know anything about each other, he doesn't know me, and I certainly don't know him.

"Challenge," he mutters. "I like that."

I roll my eyes, of course he likes a challenge the man's a fucking monster. I've heard the stories of how he'd slaughter entire families in the name of the Familiga. Then there's the whispers, Romero Bianchi is worse than the devil, the man has darkness so ingrained in him that it seeps from his pores.

I've noticed something in Romero since I came to live in the States. I've learned he's not what he seems; he is different to Dante and Alessio. That isn't what scares me, no, what has me worried about what's to come, is the fact that Romero's darkness lingers behind his eyes, and it was also present in his father's.

Matteo Bianchi was the worst of the worst. The man deserved to burn in hell for all the sins he committed.

Thank fuck he's dead. The man got off too easy for everything he did to women and children.

No one in this world is completely innocent. That's not possible. Hell fucking no. We all hold some responsibility for the atrocities that happen. I'm not clean, far from it. While I've not killed people and I never want too. I don't want to hold that guilt in my soul. I am responsible for the funding of the Irish Mafia, I'm the one they come to when they need to launder their money. I'm their go to when they need to figure out a way to get rid of real estate, or to acquire some. I know all the men and women's secrets, even though I didn't want to. But I would never tell a soul.

I'm not clean. I have my hand so far inside of the organization that I bleed it. But I won't let it take me under as it has done the rest of my family.

"What are you thinking so hard about?" He asks as he leads us to the penthouse suite.

I decide against telling him that I've heard he's a monster and switch things up. "Now you're going to be Underboss of Connecticut, will we be moving?"

He opens the door to the suite, but he keeps his eyes on me. "Do you want to move?"

I shrug. "It doesn't make a difference to me. You're the one who needs to decide what's best for you. You'll be the boss there Rome; you'll be leading the men. Would it make more sense for you to be close to them or would you prefer to stay where we are? We're married now and that means wherever you choose, I'll be by your side."

He bends at his knees and lifts me into his arms as though I weigh nothing more than a small child. I let out a surprised squeal but hold onto him for dear life. "It's a two hour drive, so if we did move, it wouldn't be as though we're across the country."

Once he has the door closed, he holds me against him as I slide down his body, his mouth gently touches mine before I pull away, and my nerves start to take over.

I turn away from him and take in the room, it's huge and so pretty. There's a beautiful bouquet on the table and some chocolates beside them along with a bottle of vodka. Seems as though Makenna knew what I would need tonight. "You don't need to decide tonight. But it's something to think about. It would also mean you're out of Dante and Makenna's shadows," I say looking back at him, addressing his statement.

His eyes narrow in on me and he stalks toward me. "You and your fucking aunt." He shakes his head, the heat in his words isn't as intense as the lust in his eyes. "Stay out of my head, Holly, you'll not like what you'll find."

I resist the urge to roll my eyes. "It's a little bit late to warn me of that, don't you think? I mean we are married, and you know as well as I do, in this life that we lead, there's no such thing as divorce."

He grits his teeth. "Not fucking happening. I'd wrap my hand around your throat and squeeze the life out of you before you even thought about leaving," he sneers.

I open my mouth to tell him to go fuck himself, but I don't get a chance. His lips are on mine as his hand goes to my hair, pulling it from the tie that's held it together all day. My hair tumbles down my back.

"Mine," he growls as he pushes away from me. "Strip," he commands, and I stare at him with a slack jaw.

He can't be fucking serious.

"I said strip and don't make me repeat myself." The hardness to his tone is matched by the stony expression he has on his face.

I reach behind me for the zipper to my dress, hating that

I'm going to have to bare myself to him. I manage to undo the zipper and the dress falls from my body and pools at my feet.

I stand before him dressed in my bra, panties, garters, and heels.

"Take it all off."

I swallow hard as I step out of my shoes, I keep my gaze on my dress as I strip out of my underwear.

"Look at me." He has this authority to his voice, one I'm unable to ignore. I raise my head and meet his gaze. His beautiful brown eyes blazing with hunger. "Fucking beautiful." He takes a step toward me and it takes every inch of control to stand my ground and not flinch. "You're perfect, Holly." His voice is hoarse. "Silky and smooth," he says as he runs his hand along my thigh. "And all fucking mine."

His hand spans the base of my back as he pulls me into his body. I crash against him and our lips meet, his tongue sweeps into my mouth and steals my breath. God, why, oh why, does he have this effect on me? Why do I want him so much?

His other hand reaches up into my hair and he tugs, the pain makes me gasp but it's not awfully painful, just enough to bite. "Lay down, I want to see you," he instructs me, and I can't deny him. Not when he speaks to me like that.

His eyes darken with lust as he takes in every inch of my naked body. My heart beats faster as he continues to stare at me, I shift slightly, needing to cover up. His gaze is too intense, his breath hot against my naked body.

"Don't hide your body from me," he growls, his voice thick and hard.

I bow my head and rest my hands at my side. The fear begins to run through my body. I have no idea what to expect. I've heard losing your virginity will hurt, it's never good for a woman their first time. But Rome has had plenty of experience and that's what frightens me the most. He knows what he's doing, what he likes and what he doesn't.

What if I do something wrong? What if he thinks I'm useless in bed?

"You have no idea how fucking sexy you look," he breathes. "Your breasts are the perfect size," he murmurs as he captures them in his hands. "Your nipples are a pale pink and yet pebbled from the cool air." His thumb runs across my right nipple and I bite back a moan.

"Tell me something, doll face, will you ignite under me like I imagine?"

His hands leave my breasts and skim down my body. My skin is on fire from his touch. I've never felt so turned on in my life. When he gets to my pussy, he licks his lips. "You're glistening already," His tongue swipes at my opening and I practically come off the bed, my back bows and I moan loudly.

"Easy, doll face, lie back and enjoy. I know I fucking will."

He continues to pleasure me and I'm squirming beneath his touch. "God, Rome," I whisper.

"I fucking love your taste, I could become addicted to it."

I close my eyes as a burning builds up inside of me. "Rome," I whisper.

"Let it happen, Hol, let it build. I want to watch you detonate." His finger attacks my clit and I'm done for, my body bows yet again as my legs begin to shake. "So, fucking responsive," he growls. "Come for me, doll face."

"Ahhhh," I cry out as my orgasm takes over me.

I blink once I'm able to compose myself and he's hovering over me, already in position to take me. The sheer determination in his eyes has me tensing. He thrusts into me, and pain explodes inside of me, making me cry out.

"Fuck, doll face, I'm sorry," he whispers to me, and I gasp as he withdraws before thrusting inside of me once again. This time though, he stays rooted inside of me. "There was no way for me not to hurt you," he tells me. "Let me know when you're adjusted to me." His hands tighten on my ass as he stills inside of me, letting the pain subside so I can get accustomed to him.

I wiggle beneath him, testing it out. When his cock thickens inside of me, I moan. No more pain. I need him. It's as though my body's burning only for him, it's only he who can extinguish this.

"Dammit," he grits out as he begins to move, slowly at first, in and out. His muscles bound tight as he keeps his weight off me.

My walls tighten around him as he continues to thrust, his movements getting faster and harder. I cling to him as I move against him, grinding as he pushes into me.

I whimper as his fingers tighten on my hips, but he doesn't stop, he doesn't relent. He thrusts into me as though he's a starved man who hasn't had his fill for years. The possessive gleam in his eyes tells me that this is more than about sex, this is about ownership. I'm his wife. Untouched, unblemished, and all his.

"Fuck," he roars as he thrusts harder than before and buries himself to the hilt inside of me. His cock expands as he releases inside of me.

MY BODY IS COMPLETELY SPENT; I don't even have the energy to raise my head. "You okay?" he asks quietly.

. . .

"YEAH, JUST LET ME SLEEP."

HIS CHUCKLE IS deep and sends shivers over my body. "Let's get you cleaned up," he says as he lifts me into his arms.

"I CAN WALK," I meekly protest, but I can't deny how good it feels to be in his arms.

HE IGNORES me and sets me onto the counter in the bathroom and uses a washcloth to clean me up. I try to take the washcloth from him, feeling awkward now we're not in bed. "Doll face, you're mine. That means every inch of you, and I take care of what's mine."

MY HEART RACES at his words. I know I shouldn't take him literally; he's already said he doesn't do love.

WHEN HE'S FINISHED, he carries me back to the bed. I'm so tired, I rest my head against his shoulder.

HE LAYS me down on the bed and slides in behind me, his front to my back as he slings an arm over me, he pulls the covers over us and I snuggle back against him.

. . .

"GOODNIGHT, ROME," I whisper, my eyes already closed and my body easing into sleep.

"NIGHT, DOLL FACE," he replies, his breath hot against my neck.

I FALL asleep thinking it's not going to take long before I fall hard for him and when I do I know that it's only going to end in heartbreak.

FOUR
ROMERO

TWO WEEKS LATER

I reach for my cell that's lying on the kitchen counter and type out a text to my men. It's time for a meeting and heads will be rolling today.

"Where's Holly?" Makenna asks me as she walks into the room.

I shrug not glancing up from my cell phone. "Haven't seen her this morning."

"What do you mean you haven't seen her this morning?" There's no missing the pissed off edge to her tone.

"She was gone before I woke up." Not that it's any of Makenna's damn business what happens between my wife and me.

I hear the front door open; I glance up and see Holly as she strolls into the kitchen wearing a sports bra and yoga pants, her body slick with sweat. Alex walks in behind her with his gaze firmly on her ass. He's part of Makenna's close security team, a solider in the Irish Mafia. Dante caved and allowed the two Mafias to mix to protect them.

"There you are," Makenna says, "I've been looking for you." She glares at Alex who is her guard and I'm wondering why he's following my wife around like a fucking puppy in heat.

"I was running, what do you need?" Holly replies, I follow her as she moves further into the kitchen, and that motherfucker's gaze hasn't moved from her ass since she walked into the room. When she bends over to reach for something in the refrigerator, I move so I'm blocking the bastard's gaze.

"Alex, time for you to leave before you die," I tell him, my voice low.

I feel Holly tense behind me but doesn't say anything. It's something I'm fucking relieved about, she never argues with me. Ever. Unlike the way Dante and Makenna are, they argue about every fucking thing. It's a headache I could do without.

Alex leaves the room not once looking back at my wife. If I see him ogling at her again, I'm not going to be held accountable for my actions. That's fucking disrespectful, I know my wife's beautiful, she's a fucking knockout, but that doesn't give a man, any man that isn't me, the right to look at her with lust in his eyes.

"What's wrong?" Her Irish accent is thick, but her words are soft and low.

"He's staring at your ass," I tell her as I spin around to face her. Her face is still red from her workout and sweat trickles from her face and down between her cleavage.

"My eyes are up here, hon," she tells me, and I can hear the smile in her voice. "And he wasn't staring at my arse."

I lift my gaze to her face, she's staring at me with barely

concealed humor. "Doll face, are you a man?" She shakes her head but narrows her eyes. "Then trust me, he was staring at your ass."

She shakes her head. "So what if he was, it doesn't mean anything."

I step closer to her, pushing her back against the refrigerator. Her eyes are wide, the vein at her neck thumps hard. "You are mine, doll face. No other man gets to taste you, no other man gets to touch you, and no other fucking man gets to look at you with lust."

She swallows hard. "Rome," she whispers, and I feel that all the way to my cock. I fucking love the way she says my name. The way her tongue rolls the R, her Irish accent makes it sound like she's saying a prayer.

I shake my head. "Nothing else to say. Next time he does it, he'll pay with his life," I promise her.

"Hon," she whispers and I'm not going to fucking lie, I love that she calls me that. Just me. "I won't ever do anything like that. A look is a look, it doesn't mean he's going to act on it, I certainly won't."

"You wouldn't survive if you even tried." For the first time, I let the full darkness seep into my words and watch as her eyes shutter close.

"Holly?" Makenna calls out and I bristle at the tone.

When Holly opens her eyes again, they're void of any emotion. "Noted," she says and moves away from me and toward her aunt. "What is it you need, Kenna?" Her voice softer when she talks to the boss.

"You'll be with me today," Makenna tells her and I grind my jaw.

My wife isn't like her, she's clean, innocent, and fucking pure from this life.

"Okay, give me thirty minutes and I'll be ready," Holly says. "Do I need anything?"

Makenna nods. "I need to find new real estate, somewhere secluded,"

Holly nods. "That's fine, anything else?"

"I also need you to talk to Maruzzo."

"No, fuck no," I say, as I step in between them.

Makenna glares at me. "Excuse you?" she replies, her tone filled with anger. "What did you say?"

"I said no. You're not going, no fucking way," I clip out, pissed Makenna's putting Holly in danger.

"Kenna," Holly says softly, "I'm going to go shower, I'll be ready in thirty." She turns to me, her eyes pleading with me. "You, follow me."

She turns on her heels and walks out of the room, not once turning back to make sure that I'm following.

"You're skating on thin fucking ice, Romero. Do not fucking question me again," Makenna snarls. "I know what Holly is capable of, what she's comfortable with. I know my niece. Do you believe I'd put her in danger?" She shakes her head in disgust. "You're dismissed." She waves her hand indicating that I should go.

I bite back my retort, having to remember this isn't just my boss, she's also my sister-in-law. The woman pisses me off unlike no other. I turn and follow my wife.

"Talk," I demand as I enter the bathroom, where she's already naked and climbing into the shower.

"What exactly would you like me to talk to you about?" she asks sweetly, and I hate that saccharine voice she has; she uses it when she's putting a wall up.

"What the fuck, Holly?" I snap, wondering why she's being so fucking childish.

She glares at me as she steps underneath the stream of

water, my body tightens as I see the water trickle down her body. "What the fuck what? You disrespected the boss, Romero. You can't do that shit. Are you that much of a fecking eejit? Christ on a bike Rome, this is the boss, what the hell is wrong with ya?" Gone is the sweet willowy voice. Her tone is harder, it has acid to it. Her accent thicker than before.

I narrow my eyes at her wondering where the fuck my sweet wife has gone? The one who never back talks me. "Wanna watch your tone?"

"No," she snaps, "I don't want to watch my fucking tone. You married me knowing who my family is."

"You're fucking innocent," I roar. "You stay the fuck out of our business."

She blinks, the anger dissipating from her. "You think I'm innocent? I'm far fucking from it. I may not have killed anyone, but Rome, I'm so far into this life, I bleed it. It's who I am, who I have always been."

"Bullshit," I fire back. "You don't fucking bleed for us, no more."

She shakes her head as she reaches for her loofah. "Hon, I love that you think that, but you and I both know that's not true. I'll bleed for this family, just the scars we bear are different. Yours are deeper and embedded in you and have been for a long time. Mine, well I pray every day I don't get sucked into the darkness."

That's never fucking going to happen. "You're pure, doll face, you're not like the rest of us," I say, as I start to strip out of my clothes.

Her eyes widen. "No, Rome, I don't have time."

I shrug, like I give a fuck. "You're mine doll face, which means I can fuck you whenever I want to." I step into the shower and she immediately moves toward me, her loofah abandoned. As much as she'd like to pretend she's pissed, she wants me as much as I want her.

I lift her into my arms, and she wraps her legs around my waist, "Rome," she whispers when I push into her. Her arms go around my shoulder where she holds on tight, "God, you feel so fucking good."

I move so that her back is pressed against the wall and thrust hard into her. Biting back a groan as I hit deep inside of her. Fuck, her pussy is so fucking tight.

I never thought I'd be this guy, the one that would want to be with the same woman every night. But knowing this woman is mine and only mine has ignited something inside of me, something primal. I don't love Holly, hell nowhere fucking near, that's not who I am. But I care for her, probably as much as I care for my brothers. I'd take a bullet for her just as I would for them.

"Rome," she groans as she tightens around my cock, "ah," she cries as she detonates. I press my mouth against hers swallowing her cries as I thrust harder, my balls tighten as I plant myself inside of her and come.

I rest my forehead against her breasts as I regain my breath. "You need me, doll face, call me," I tell her.

Her arms around me spasm. "Hey, this still isn't about me going to see Maruzzo is it?"

I lift my head and glare at her. "The man is a fucking monster," I snarl, pissed she's acting as though going to see that motherfucker isn't anything out of the ordinary.

Her hand brushes against my face and I still. "It's what I do," she says softly, "I'm the money girl, Rome, I'm the one who makes sure you all stay out of jail, I'm the one who makes sure you're all above board and legit. So yes, sometimes I must go and see these arseholes who believe I'm stupid and not worth their time, but they have to deal with it as I'm the one that's in charge of most of their finances."

"I still don't like it." I hate she has to deal with this shit, she should be untarnished, pure as the day I married her.

"You don't have to, this is what I do, it's what I've always done. I now work for Dante and Makenna, just as you do. I'm glad I don't have to see the shit you do." She unwinds her legs from my waist, and I pull out of her. She moves down my body until her feet touch the ground. "I'm now running late and Kenna's going to be pissed." She gripes as she stands back under the stream of water.

"We really need to move." I sigh as I reach for her loofah.

"Told you, hon, whatever you want. I'm surprised you hadn't suggested it before. It would be so much easier for you, you'd be home earlier, you'd be closer to your men. You wouldn't have to live in a house with your brothers."

Ain't that the motherfucking truth. Since Holly and I have been married, Alessio's been even more annoying than usual. He's taking risks he shouldn't be taking. Dante tells me to leave him be, he's making a foothold for himself in a world where he never had one before. But gambling? That's something that could go fucking wrong if he tangles with the wrong man.

"What about you?" I ask as I wash her body, "Wouldn't you be more comfortable here?"

"It doesn't bother me. I'm used to being alone. I mean Da was busy with work and the kids were at school or the nanny had them. Ma, well, she was off doing whoever she liked. I'm not real comfortable around a lot of people, I'm more of an introvert." she gives me a smile, one that has my cock stirring again. "But ultimately, if we were to move, Alessio wouldn't annoy me or you, Makenna and Dante will have to call on someone else to sort their shit out." I raise my brow at her words. She doesn't care though, she merely shrugs, "I love Kenna, but since we married, you've done everything for them both, and that's not fair to you. You'd never complain because that's not you. However, you have men who need your time, and Rome, you can't keep dividing your time between the four of us."

"What you're saying is that if we move, I'll have more time for you?" I can't keep the bite out of my tone, I thought she knew this. I thought she fucking understood.

She narrows her eyes at me, but I'm not finished.

"When did you begin to think you mattered enough to me to give you that much time?"

She clenches her jaw. "You're right. You never did." Her lips twist into a scowl. "Decide what you want to do and when you have, let me know." She reaches behind her and switches off the shower.

I watch on with a clenched jaw as she grabs a towel and wraps it around her body. Her eyes void of emotion and she's not once glanced at me. Any progress we made in the past two weeks, I've just fucking killed.

Fuck.

When she walks out of the bathroom, I turn the shower back on. I can't help but wonder what this means for us now.

Twenty minutes later and she's fully dressed. "I've got to go," she tells me as I pull on my shirt. "I'll see you later."

"What time will you be home?" I have no fucking idea why the hell I'm asking her that.

She merely shrugs. "I don't know, I'm not sure how long this will last. Have dinner without me. I'm sure your brothers would love to catch up." She glances at her cell phone. "I've got to go, bye." She walks out of the door and doesn't look back.

"TELL ME," I say menacingly. Pissed the fuck off that these assholes are still being fucking childish and thinking they can get me to leave. "Why are you still playing these games? I am not a man to be trifled with. I'm not going fucking anywhere. My wife is one of you and therefore, I am family. I will protect you if you show loyalty and I have no fucking qualms in taking you out if you don't. Now, does anyone have anything to fucking say?"

The men stand taller, each time we have a meeting I see the respect start to grow, I don't have as many naysayers as I did at the beginning, I'm proving myself to them. I'm out on the streets with them, I'm not hiding behind the status of Underboss, that's just not who I am; it wasn't ingrained in me. I'm a man who needs to be in the thick of it, to be in the action.

"The next time we have a meeting and someone, any fucking one shows disrespect, it'll be the last thing you do. Do I make myself clear?" I say loud enough to be heard. I have almost thirty men working for me and the number is growing. The younger generation who wasn't sure about my predecessor are suddenly interested, they know me from my reputation alone and they want that, they want to work with a man who can kill without breaking a sweat or batting an eyelid.

Fuck. Killing doesn't affect me at all. My mom told me that it was because I'm broken, that my father's evil had seeped into me and broke me until I became a monster. Her words struck a chord with me since I was seven and she saw me with the knife and gun, bloodied, with dead men at my feet.

I never understood why she was crying, never could

figure out why me killing two men who had broken into our home trying to kill her to get at my father was such a bad thing. I thought I had done the right thing, but as I grew up and I listened to the rest of the made men as they recanted their first kills and how they felt, I realized my mom was right. I'm more like my father than I care to admit.

"Boss," Jason says as I exit the warehouse. "We've got a problem," he begins.

Of fucking course we have a problem, I'm a motherfucking Italian who's the Underboss of the Irish mafia. We've always had a problem.

"Anderson's on his way to the hospital, took two to the chest from a drive by."

Fuck. Anderson is one of the loyal men, he's loyal to the family and therefore he supports me as I'm married to the great-granddaughter of the original Clann leader.

"Who?" I ask, my voice vibrating with anger.

"I have Layton checking the security feeds around the store at the time of the shooting."

"Where did it happen?"

"Granny Jones's." His teeth clenched as are his fists. Granny Jones is a restaurant owned by the Irish Mafia, it's a front to run the money through. It's in New York City and I'm curious as to why Anderson was there and not here where he was due to be. Especially as I had called a meeting.

"Who else was there? Any of the other men injured?"

He glances away and I wait, knowing he hasn't told me everything. "No boss, none of the other men were injured. Your wife was present at the time of the shooting. She wasn't shot, boss, but she was close to where the bullets were."

I don't even listen to anything else he's saying, my feet are pushing me toward my fucking car.

I've made my fucking mind up. We're moving. I have two fucking hours to drive before I can get to her. No more. Where I go, she goes. She fucking said it. We're moving and that's that.

FIVE
HOLLY

"Tell me again," Kenna says as she shoves the cup into my hands. "And for God's sake, drink the bloody tea."

I wrap my hands around the cup hoping the warmth will take away the coldness that seeped into my body and hasn't let go since. "Makenna," I say softly, "I'm not sure how much more I can tell you." I'm tired, I want to go take a shower and wash this blood off me. The shooting happened almost two hours ago and I'm tired, sore, and emotional.

"For my sake, please, walk me through what happened," she asks as she perches on the corner of the coffee table in front of me.

"I met with Maruzzo like you wanted. At first he was the same as always..." I begin and a shiver runs through my body. I bring the cup to my lips and take a sip, the cut on my lip stings as the heat hits it but I ignore it and drink.

"In what way was he the same as always?" Now this is new, she hasn't asked me this question before.

I shrug as I bring my legs up onto the sofa, putting the soles of my feet flat against the material and rest my forearms on my thigh. "He's an arsehole, Kenna, he hates that

I'm a woman and the one who deals with money. Whenever I have to deal with him, he's disrespectful, either staring at my tits or he's not looking at me at all. Then there's the way he talks to me, as though I'm merely a piece of shit beneath his shoe. It's fine, whatever, I'm used to it, so I don't work as hard in putting his money into the right stocks."

It's something I learned straight off the bat, men, especially the men in the Mafia; they're all the same. All they care about is money and status. The more money you have, the more respect it garners and that could mean a promotion if the men respect you that much. With Maruzzo and the other men like him, I make sure they make enough to keep them satisfied but not enough to put them in the category that my friends and family are in. We're all wealthy, obscenely so, but we don't flaunt it.

"Right," she says. "So what happened then?"

Before I answer her, Dante walks into the room a scowl fixed onto his face. "That was Romero, he's on his way back, he's pissed and demanding answers."

"Yeah, well he's not the only one," Makenna fires back. My aunt is a force to be reckoned with when she's pissed.

"We were talking about where his money should go next, as in what property to buy to expand the 'legitimate' side to his business." I use finger quotes for legitimate because we all know there's no such thing. The made men buy up stores, shopping malls, banks, and restaurants under the pretense that they're actual businessmen when in fact, they do it to keep the police off their backs.

"Apparently, the men had been talking." I glance at Dante, that's a big fucking no-no. You don't talk about what I do for you, just as I don't say what the boss' plans are. It's the reason why I'm able to continue to do what I do. "He wanted a more lucrative purchase. Money I know he shouldn't be able to get without refinancing some of his other businesses, which he has no intention of doing." Which means he's stashing his money and that will lead to questions like why is he doing it? Where is the money coming from? Then it'll go to is he a traitor and we all know what happens to traitors in the family.

"I'll have the men look into it," Dante assures me and I'm wondering if that's the right thing to do or not, but he's the boss and I bite my tongue. It's one thing to criticize them in front of my husband and it's a different thing to do so to their faces.

"We'll look into it," Kenna insists, not glancing at her husband for approval. "So, he was interested in expanding, so you were talking, then what happened?"

"I reached for my coffee and then there were gunshots, six or seven at first, the windows smashed, and I threw myself down onto the bench until the shooting stopped." I remember sitting up and seeing the destruction all around me. "When I got to my feet, Anderson was on the floor and Maruzzo was gone."

I'm not sure when he managed to slip away but he did, and the fucker didn't even check to see if everyone was okay.

Makenna and Dante share a look, and I know what it means. Either Maruzzo was in on the hit or he was the one they were aiming for, and if it wasn't him, who was the intended target, then who was, and that could lead back to me.

"Are we done?" I ask her, needing to get away.

She nods. "Yeah, Hols, go on up and have a shower. I'll check on you in a bit," she says softly.

I get to my feet and watch as she gently caresses her

stomach. She's three months pregnant and yet she's not even showing.

I slowly make my way up the stairs, my bare feet getting colder by the second as I make my way toward mine and Romero's room. This house is too small, we're all practically on top of each other. Makenna and Dante have purchased another home that they had intended on being in before Rome and I got married but when they found out Makenna was expecting, they wanted changes made to the house so when the baby arrived it would be as safe as the white house.

I turn on the shower as soon as I enter the bathroom. Tears slowly start to leak from my eyes. Today has been shit. From the moment I woke up, it's just been fucking crap. Mal texted me this morning, Ma's on the warpath, she thinks Da's found himself a woman. I say fucking fair play to him. He can't be expected to stay celibate for the rest of his life. But Ma hates to share and of course I don't answer her calls, in fact, I have her number blocked. So, she calls Mal hoping to get him onside, but she fucked up when she told him Da wasn't his biological dad.

Then there was Alessio, that fucker is pissed about the porn magazines I have sent to him monthly. That was Makenna's idea but still, I'm the one to blame and he constantly glares and growls at me whenever I'm alone with him. It's come to the point where I'll leave any room he's in so I don't have to listen to him bitch about me or even glare at me.

Then the shit with Romero happened. God, just when I thought we were making progress we were finally starting to get somewhere, he pulls back and erects a fifty-foot wall between us. I knew he could be callous, that his darkness was there, always bubbling on the surface. I was naive, I thought he wouldn't hurt me. But sometimes words hurt more than any slap, punch, or kick does.

The tears stream down my face as I step into the boiling hot shower, the water beats against my back, the steam filling the room. I can't stop the tears as my body wracks with sobs. I sink to the bottom of the shower and wrap my arms around my knees as I cry my heart out.

Of course, that's how Romero finds me, I'm not sure how long I've been sitting here but I'm lifted into his arms and I face plant into his neck, my hands tightening around him as I cry some more. He doesn't say a word, just holds me tight.

"Your clothes are getting wet," I murmur against him once my crying jag finishes.

"Don't care," he says as he puts me back down on my feet. Hurt slashes through me but I bite my lip to stop the whimper from coming out. His thumb gently pulls my lip from between my teeth, his eyes darkening as he takes in the cut. "This happen at the restaurant?"

I nod, unable to speak right now as his hands run over my body. I'm so confused, I have no idea what's going on.

"Are you hurt anywhere else?"

"I don't think so," I whisper.

"The adrenaline," he says as he steps closer to me, his gaze going over my body. When he takes my hand into his, he turns it over and I see there's cuts on it. "Finish your shower, doll face, then I'll see to the cuts."

"What?" I whisper, wondering what happened between earlier and now. It's as though it's two different people, that or he has a split personality.

I'm speechless as he gently washes me, every inch of me, including my hair. He places kisses against my neck, mouth, and head as he does so. I'm so confused. I'm unable to think clearly with him being this close to me.

"Come on doll face," he whispers as he lifts me into his arms and out of the shower. He reaches for a towel and wraps me in it, the warmth finally starting to make its way into my body. "I've got you," he tells me and I'm once again, so close to tears. He reaches for another towel and I can't take it anymore; the tenderness is unlike anything I've ever experienced. I feel as though I'm wide open and he can see every single scar I've been left with. I hate it. I hate I don't know him, that I'm falling in love with a man who just wants me for sex and ownership.

I'm scared I'm going to turn bitter and twisted like my mother. She loved my dad, adored him, until she realized her feelings would never be reciprocated and in a sense she lost herself and who she really was. So, she became this woman I have no love or respect for. That's someone I don't want to become, so twisted with rage that she'll lash out at those closest to her because she feels the need to hurt someone so she's not alone.

He throws a towel onto the bed and sits me down onto it. My heart constricts with so much emotion. I know I'm not like my family. I'm unable to bury everything deep down below. Sometimes, my emotions bleed out of me, just as they are now.

Whatever he sees has him taking my face in his hands and kissing me so fucking softly. I hate he's got this power over me. I have no idea what the power is, but it's a force to be reckoned with. "Never again," he promises me. "No one will ever hurt you again."

I shake my head. "You can't promise me that," I tell him. There's no way he can. Not after today, not after his words. Remembering them is like a punch to my gut, all the anger from this morning is back in full force.

"I fucking can," he growls, his hands tightening around

my face. The look in his eyes is determination and something else, one I haven't witnessed Romero have before.

"No, hon, you can't. Especially when you're the one who hurts me the most." I pull away from him and start to dry myself off, I need to get out of this frame of mind. The vulnerable, scared, wimpy girl. I know better than to be this girl. Better than to lean on anyone for support. Ma taught me that at a young age. She taught me so many lessons and yet, here I am, forgetting the golden one.

Men will always hurt you. Never let them in. Never give them the power to succeed.

"Holly," his voice is gruff, "about what I said this morning..."

I turn to face him. "Did you mean what you said?"

He's silent, and that's the only answer I need. He meant every fucking word. Each single letter was a slice to my heart.

Stupid, naive Holly. I should have known being with Romero would only lead to heartache. I mean, look at how we started off. A fucking trade off. He becomes the Underboss and gets a wife all in one go. What do I get? A broken heart and a husband who doesn't care.

I get dressed into some sweats, not once looking at Romero; I can't do it, I know if I turn and see that he has that fucking look on his face, the one that's filled with such tenderness, I'll cave and let him hold me. That's stupid on my part. Having Romero touch me is dangerous. He makes me want things I can't have, hope for things that aren't possible.

I walk out of our bedroom, and I can hear voices downstairs. I sigh, not in the mood for company and I know Makenna will hover if I'm around her. I make my way into the library, and where each wall is covered in books from floor to ceiling. This is a room which I spend a lot of time in, no one else uses it. I move over to the oversized chair and climb into it, curling up into a ball. I reach for the blanket and pull it over me as my other hand reaches for my e-reader. There's nothing better after an emotional day than reading a book.

I need to escape, to find a void away from my life and right now the only way to do that is to read. I power up the e-reader and spend a few minutes browsing books before I settle upon one.

It's not long before my eyes start to droop. The events of today have taken their toll. I hope tomorrow brings a better day. Within minutes I'm fast asleep.

SIX
ROMERO

I drove like a mad man to get home. I've never felt helpless before and that's exactly what I was feeling as I drove the two fucking hours to get to her. I walked into the house and the first thing I asked was, "Where is she?" Makenna didn't hesitate in telling me that Holly went for a shower. Walking into the bathroom and seeing my wife sobbing on the shower floor cracked yet another fucking piece of my heart.

Holly, although she's sweet and soft, she's fucking strong. She never shows weakness to anyone and yet I've seen her at her most vulnerable. Knowing I hurt her with my words from this morning stings, but I need her to realize that this marriage isn't based on love. I can see it when she looks at me, that she's starting to develop feelings and the more I let that continue the more she'll fall and as much as I'm a bastard, I'm not that type of fucking monster to break my wife.

"Is Holly okay?" Makenna asks as I walk into the kitchen.

I look at my sister-in-law. She's different in this house compared to how she is outside. Here she freely shows that she gives a fuck about those closest to her, whereas outside, she's the boss, she'll break every bone in your body if you piss her off. Right now, though, Makenna's pale and pacing. That doesn't bode well.

"Yeah," I lie knowing she'd hate for me to tell them she was crying. Makenna narrows her eyes as though she doesn't believe me. "What happened?" I demand, needing to know who the fuck to kill for even thinking about doing a drive by shooting anywhere near my wife.

Makenna and Dante share a look, one which has me bracing. Fuck. What the hell haven't they told me?

"What?" I ground out. "Fucking tell me." I snap, as Alessio strolls into the room.

"Someone," Makenna snarls, her eyes fixed on my little brother, "has been running their mouth about the shit Holly does for them."

"Marisa found out about the investments she's made for the other Italian made men since she's been here," Dante says, his arms crossed over his chest. "So, Alessio, want to tell me what you've told him?" Maruzzo is the father of Alessio's friend, Maxim, he's an asshole who's just like his father.

He shrugs. "I told them she makes me a lot of money."

"Before we get any further," Makenna's voice is hard and filled with anger, "let me make myself fucking clear." She steps up to him and Alessio's eyes widen, she's never spoken this way to him before. "Carry on your fucking shit and I'll end you. I do not care that you are Dante's brother. Holly is my niece and I'll do whatever the hell I have to in order to protect her. If my brother finds out how you've been treating his daughter, there's no fucking place on this earth that you'll be able to hide from him."

Her words hit me. "What the fuck have you done to my wife?"

"She shouldn't have signed me up to that shit," he snarls his eyes darting between Makenna and me.

"You're a fucking eejit," Makenna tells him as she slaps him on the back of the head. "She did it on my say so. You have a fucking problem with that, then come to me. You do not fucking call her a bitch and you do not make her uncomfortable in her home."

"Yes boss," he replies, and she nods seemingly okay with his answer.

Fuck no. That's not okay. I'm going to fucking kill him. "We'll be having words later." Why the hell didn't she tell me that Alessio was being a dick to her? He doesn't get to call her a bitch. Ever.

He clenches his jaw but nods.

"So, what have you been telling Maxim and Maruzzo?" Dante asks, his voice is deceptively calm, yet we all know differently, the way his jaw clenches and narrowing of his eyes, he's pissed and I'm getting angrier the longer I'm left in the dark.

"I only told Max a few things Holly had in the pipeline for me," he shrugs as though it's not a big deal. "I mean that's why she's here right?" The dismissive way he's talking about her makes me want to wrap my fingers around his neck and break it. He turns his gaze to me, "Come on, even you have to agree with me."

"Holly isn't here to work for you," I snap, pissed he's even talking this way about her. "She's here because she's my wife. You may be my brother, Alessio, but make no mistake about who I am. I'll not hesitate in carving your heart out from your chest."

His eyes widen as he turns to Dante, as though he's

seeking his help. "You fucked up, Ales, at least have the balls to own up to it. Holly is family, she helped you because you are family. Now, what have you told Maruzzo and Maxim?"

"They know she's able to hide money as well as property."

"You fucking arsehole!" Makenna screams. "Do you realize what you've done?"

"What? She can do those things," he says as he glances between the three of us.

"Yes, she can, and she stays out of this life, Alessio, she's kept hidden because she knows everyone's fucking secrets, she knows who's skimming from the family and who's getting money from outside sources. Yet, Maruzzo demanded another meeting with her," Makenna explains. "Do you know what happened while she was at that meeting?"

"What happened?" he asks and he's finally realizing why what Holly does is supposed to stay secret. Why you don't brag about the shit she does for you.

"There was a drive by shooting. What Holly doesn't know, and I won't be fucking telling her, is that she was the intended target," Dante casually announces.

I spin and face my brother, my boss, my anger is palpable.

"I know you're pissed, Rome, I'd be fucking pissed too if the tables were reversed. But I need you to beat it back."

"Fuck that," Makenna says as she stands beside her husband. "I say let Romero unleash his demon. I mean, if the tables were reversed and it was me that was in Granny Jones', there's no way you'd listen to anyone who told you to rein in your temper."

He sighs, "That may be so, but the way I feel for you is different than what Rome feels for Holly."

"So, he doesn't love her, that doesn't mean he doesn't care about her," she fires back, and I know if I don't step in, these two are going to be arguing and then they'll move to their bedroom and I need answers.

"Why," I ask, cutting through their hushed tones. "Why should I beat it back?"

Makenna's right. I do care about Holly. I shouldn't. Fuck, I shouldn't have been able to marry her. I can destroy her, shatter her into a million pieces and yet, I know she's the only woman that I'd ever care about.

"Because Maruzzo is on the run, as is Maxim," Dante announces, his eyes narrowed in on Alessio. "Innocent people don't run, your job, Ales, and your only fucking job right now is to find out where they've gone."

"Why would they do this?" he says, swallowing hard. He knows that he's fucked up when it comes to his treatment of Holly, the guilt is shining in his eyes. But I don't give a fuck. He shouldn't be treating my wife with anything but respect. Now he's realized just how much he's truly fucked up.

"Because Maruzzo Damini worked with your father and has been in constant contact with Kurt," Makenna tells us and my jaw clenches. Kurt and my father organized with the Bratva to do a fucking shootout at Dante and Makenna's wedding. Alessio was shot in his gut while Makenna's arm was grazed. Since then, Kurt's been in the fucking wind. Melissa, Holly's sister-in-law who's a hacker, had tracked him to Chicago. But he's been in the wind ever since. It's like tracing a fucking ghost, how can one man hide from two fucking families? And yet, he's doing just that.

"So, Ales, your job, and your only fucking job right now is to find out what the fuck those Damini men are up to, where they're hiding and what they have planned," Dante snarls, his jaw tight as he glares at our brother. He shakes his head and walks out of the room, I've never seen Dante this pissed at Alessio before, he's usually the good boy.

"He wants you to be his consigliere," Makenna begins, her voice vibrating with anger. "What you've done," she shakes her head, "you're an asshole, Alessio. Not only have you broken the trust your brother had in you. That your boss had in you. You've put one of ours at risk." She moves toward him. "Anything happens to Holly and I don't give a fuck that you're family, I'll kill you." Her words clipped and filled with promise. "Fix this," she demands pinning him with one last glare before turning and following her husband.

"Rome..." he begins but I shake my head, my jaw clenched, right now, I'm too fucking angry to listen to his bullshit excuses. "I didn't realize."

I take a step back and stand against the wall, needing to put distance between us so I don't fucking kill him. "Didn't realize what? That what Holly does means she could be a target? Or that you called her a bitch?"

"No one fucking talked about the shit she does, how was I supposed to know?"

I scoff. "Are you for fucking real? We don't talk about it because what she does is illegal and if our enemies found out, she'd be their fucking target. Jesus, Ales, seriously, you cannot be this fucking stupid."

He glances down at his feet. "I'm sorry, Rome, honest, I had no idea."

"Fuck," I grit out, pissed that Holly's in danger. I guess now it's time to find out what the hell is up with him. "What the fuck is wrong with you, Ales? Since Holly's been here you've changed."

He shakes his head, "It's not Holly, I actually like her."

"Then what? You've been acting like a fucking asshole. You're gambling away all the money you have. Why?"

"Dad," is all he says.

"What about him?" That motherfucker is dead, I wish I had the chance to kill him, but unfortunately, I didn't get the chance, that honor was left to Dante. I was, however, lucky enough to get a front row seat to his demise. It was glorious to watch as the life left his eyes. It's a fucking shame the fucker didn't suffer, he deserved to for all he did to us all.

"He's dead, I should be fucking glad. I should be happy, ecstatic, overjoyed and yet whenever any of the men talk about him, they talk about this fierce leader who led them. A man they respected. Someone they all looked up to and aspired to emulate."

My lips turn up in disgust. "Fuck, no, that's bullshit, and you know it."

He glances at me, and I remember the little six-year-old boy who sat at our father's feet as he slaughtered two men. He watched on as our father tore the skin from their faces because of some slight he thought they did against him. Since that day, Alessio changed, he was darker, and I knew he would do anything our father asked without question. Whereas our father knew there were limits to what Dante and I would do without delving deeper.

Growing up I knew my father hated me, I didn't give a fuck. I hated him back just as hard, maybe even harder. I never had respect for a man that could beat the crap out of his wife and rape women and barely legal girls. But I knew my place, I had to show respect for him. He was the boss, the capo. It was demanded I give him respect, and if I didn't, it was a sure fire way of getting myself killed.

"Is it?" His words are clipped. "Then why the hell are all

those men, our men, so fucking upset that the bastard's dead? Why do they give a fuck that he's buried six feet under where he fucking belongs?"

"Because," I say slowly, I'm pissed he's even talking about this shit. "The men haven't gotten with the times. The Famiglia isn't the Clann. We Italian's, our women are different. They do not get involved in our business. But not only is Dante younger than a lot of our men, his wife is the boss of the Irish Mafia. They don't like it so they're grumbling about shit that's not even true. Wise the fuck up, Alessio. Before you fuck your life up or anyone else's."

He sighs, his hand swiping at his stubble. "They say I'm like him. That out of the three of us, I'm the one who's like him."

Finally, the fucking truth. "You may look like him, you may have the same fucking temper as him, but the difference between you and him is you'd never harm a woman the way he did. You'd never harm your children as he did." I finally step away from the wall and move toward him. "You need to fucking sort yourself out before you lose everything."

His hands go to his hair and he pulls tightly. His face etched in pain. "Fuck. Holly." He gasps and takes a step toward the door. I put my hand on his chest. "I need to apologize."

"Yeah, you fucking do. But not now. Do you honestly think I'd let you anywhere near her right now? Especially after the way you've been treating her?" I ask with a raised brow. "She's been through enough today. You can apologize tomorrow."

He nods and leaves the room. For the first time in months, I finally see my brother again.

This life can consume you. You have a choice. You can

let it suck you in and destroy you, or you can grow from it, become stronger. This life shows us the weak from the strong. The way Alessio was going, I thought he'd be one of the ones life sucked up and spat out. Now, well now, I hope he shows the world how much like our father he truly is. No one fucks with this family and gets away with it. It's time Alessio showed the world how fucking fierce he is.

I reach for the pop tarts in the pantry and toast a few. My mind's running, as I try to come up with the best way to protect Holly. She could have been seriously fucking injured today.

"She's in the library," Makenna tells me as I pass by her for the second time. I've been searching for my wife and I've checked the entire house and yet, can't find her anywhere.

"There's a library?" Dante asks, looking up from his laptop.

Makenna sighs. "Yes, there's a library, and it's obvious only Holly uses it." She tells me where it is. "Are you going to tell her about today?"

"I've thought about it." I don't want any harm coming to her. She means something to me. Her vulnerability shines like a beacon to me and I want to protect her at all costs. "At the moment, she's to be kept in the dark. I don't want her worrying."

Makenna nods. "I agree. Just don't fuck this up, Romero."

I give her a glare. When it comes to my work, to the family she is the boss. But when it comes to my life. To my fucking wife, she has no say whatsoever.

I turn and make my way toward the library, when I reach the door, I push it open, fully expecting to get the cold shoulder once again, but instead I find my beautiful wife curled up in the chair fast asleep. Damn, she looks so fucking peaceful.

She doesn't know it, but she's dug herself deep inside of me. I'm not a man that shows emotions. But Holly, well she's come into my life and burrowed her way through my walls. I'll be fucking damned if I let anyone hurt her. I'm going to tear the world down to find out where those fucking Damini assholes are. They'll not get the chance to try and finish the job.

SEVEN

HOLLY

ONE MONTH LATER

"You okay?" Alex asks me as I push harder as we turn the corner, I'm almost there. Almost home. My legs are burning but I ignore the pain and keep going. "Hol, what's going on?" His breath coming out in pants.

I shrug. "I have no idea what you're talking about. There's nothing going on." What a fucking lie that is. I'm being kept in the dark about something, I can feel it. Every time I walk into a room where Romero, Makenna, and Dante are they all stop talking.

"Bullshit," he replies, and I roll my eyes. He's got something to say, Alex doesn't know when to keep his mouth closed. He hates Romero and I'm not sure why. I push harder, sprinting the last hundred meters.

"Holly, the past month you've been acting weird," he says as his fingers clamp around my wrist and he pulls me to a stop. "Every day you push yourself harder and harder. Talk to me," he pleads with me.

I swallow harshly, being around Alex used to be okay, he was fun to be around, and he'd make me laugh, but lately it's been weird. He's giving me lingering looks and always finds a reason to stand close to me. "I'm fine," I say through clenched teeth as I wrench my arm away from him. "What the hell?" I exclaim, wondering if he's lost his ever loving mind?

Each morning I go for a run and Alex is always the one to go with me. Whenever I'm in the house, he's there, hovering. It's really started to freak me out. Today will be the last day that I go running, I'll have to find another way to keep fit.

"What the hell?" he repeats. "Come on Holly, you can't be that naive? Romero doesn't love you. He used you to get his position."

I glare at him. "You don't think I know that?" I snap, pissed that we're even having this conversation.

I'm reminded of the fact that my husband doesn't love me each and every day. Nighttime comes around and he's the most attentive lover in the world. But as soon as morning rolls around, he's cold, distant, and acts as though I'm merely an inconvenience. It's gotten to the point now where I steer clear of him during the day.

When I left Ireland, I promised myself I'd never be the woman that my ma is or the woman she turned me into. The one that was treated as though I wasn't wanted. I've tried to steel my heart against the rejection that Romero heaps on me, I've tried to not let it get to me. I want to be better, be better than the woman I had as a role model.

"Why the hell are you with him?" Alex demands to know as he steps into my personal space. "Why, Hol? Why stick with it, you deserve better. You deserve more than a loveless marriage."

"Leave it alone Alex. My marriage has nothing to do with you." I turn, not wanting to discuss this any longer. Alex is out of line.

"You should have someone who will worship you, who'll show you what it's like to be loved," he says and my body tenses, he can't be fucking serious. I spin on my heel and see the truth written all over his face.

"Alex," I whisper. "No matter what, Romero is my husband. You are a soldier, if you continue this shit, you're going to lose your life. Do you want that?"

I'm not Ma, I've taken my vows; I'd never cheat on my husband. I know what it means, death. Ma's lucky that she hasn't eaten a bullet yet. But I suppose she knows that and why she keeps getting pregnant. Da wasn't sure about Chloe being his, but when Mary came along, there was no way he could deny the truth any longer. Da has six children, only two are biologically his.

"Fuck that," he bites out. "You deserve to be treated like the princess that you are." He reaches out to touch me and I dodge it, he's not touching me. Not now, not ever. "Holly?"

I glare at the man that I thought was my friend. "I can't believe you," I hiss. "How dare you? Romero is my husband, Alex. Mine. You don't like him, that's on you. But don't bring me into whatever fucking twisted game you're playing."

His jaw clenches, "I'm not playing a game. I want you. You shouldn't have to be treated as though you don't matter."

"I fucking matter." I don't give a shit if Romero doesn't love or care about me. I care about myself. I matter to so many people. To people that I love.

"You really want to stay here and be with that asshole?" he questions.

I stand taller, I square my shoulders and glare at him. "I'm only going to say this once more. So, listen to me." I snap at him, pissed that he's making me out to be some sort of weak woman when I'm not. "I knew what I was getting into when I agreed to marry Romero. I knew that it would be a loveless marriage and that Romero was doing it to cement his place within the higher ranks of not only the Irish Mafia but also the Italian. But he is my husband. You do not get to judge us." I give him one last glare. "Stay the fuck away from me."

I hear his deep sigh as I walk away. I'm not giving him any more of my time. I've told him what I want, and he'd better listen otherwise I'm going to say something to Makenna.

Of course, when I move toward the door, Romero, Dante, Alessio, and Makenna are standing there, the men with pissed off looks on their faces while Makenna's got a smirk on hers. "Enjoy eavesdropping?" I ask as I push past them and into the house.

"You've got a choice," I hear Makenna begin, "you either go and work for Finn, or you're done."

"Fuck." The guttural curse from Alex makes my heart clench. He was my friend, he loved working for the bosses. But he fucked up. He should have never said a word to me about my marriage. He should have never crossed that line. That's on him, yet I somehow feel responsible.

"Come near my wife again and I'll slit your fucking throat." Romero's threat is the last thing I hear before I walk into my bedroom and close the door, I need a shower. My gut is churning, I know that Romero's going to have something to say about this morning's antics. I'm not in the mood to listen to it.

Two hours later and I'm sitting on the kitchen counter eating pop tarts. They're something that I didn't eat while in Ireland but since I moved here, they're one of my favorite foods.

"How the hell can you eat that shit?" Makenna asks as reaches into the fridge for some pop. "I swear you and Romero are made for each other."

I roll my eyes, "Yeah, sure." I mutter, "what's the plan for today?"

She grins at me. "You always were my favorite."

I glare at her which makes her grin wider. "You're a bloody liar, Makenna Gallagher-Bianchi. A God damn liar. Out of all your siblings, you prefer Finn. Then out of your nephews, it's Danny."

She nods. "That is true, but you are my favorite niece, and out of my cousins, I'd pick Hayden."

"Whatever," I mutter, "have you spoken to Hayden recently?" I'm still pissed at my Aunt Edwina, she didn't come to the wedding, nor did Killian.

"No, but I have spoken to Killian, he's with them, or he was last week. Something about Annemarie being a bitch." Annemarie is married to Hayes, our other cousin. Aunt Edwina's eldest son, who's a bloody moron.

"Knew that," I say quietly which has Makenna laughing. "What, we all knew that. I swear the Gallagher's have something missing or broken in our DNA, we all go for complete and utter arseholes. There's our Ma's, not to mention that cow Annemarie."

Makenna nods. "Yep, the women are bitches and the men we marry are bastards." Oops, seems as though there's trouble in paradise, then again, the way these two bicker, it's almost foreplay.

I lift my coffee cup. "Amen to that." I salute her and she giggles. "So, what's Annemarie done now?" I ask, as the men walk into the kitchen.

Makenna grins as she hops up onto the counter opposite me.

Dante glares at us both. "Do you have to sit there? I make food there."

I raise a brow. "I make the food," I remind him, as the housekeeper that Makenna had, is now gone, she stayed for a while but as they're moving, she decided to retire. "I also wash down the counters, so I can put my arse wherever the hell I want."

Makenna nods. "It's my house. I can do what I want."

Romero stalks over to me and snatches the box of pop tarts from my hands. "Hey!" I cry as I reach for them again. The tricky bastard already stole one. "Get your own."

He grins at me and it reaches his eyes, my heart stutters at the sight. Damn it. Why does he affect me this way? "What's yours is mine," he tells me, and I stick my tongue out at him. I've learned there's no point in arguing with him. He's a caveman and just shuts me down no matter what I say. I'm pretty sure he's born a couple of centuries too late.

"So," I say, ignoring the heat in my husband's eyes. "What did the bitch do this time?" I ask Makenna again.

She grins. "Get this," she begins, and I know that whatever it is, isn't going to be good. "She told Aunt Edwina that she wished that she had never gotten married to Hayes."

"She should have kept her legs closed then," I say as Romero snatches the box from my hands again. "Will you quit it? I'm hungry." I whine and turn to face him to see him staring at me with his lips slightly parted, his eyes are wide, and he's got a cheeky grin on his face. "What?"

Makenna's smiling as she glances around at the men, they're all looking at me as though they've never seen me before. "What the hell is wrong with you three?" she questions.

"I've just never heard Holly say something so..." Alessio begins, and I grin, he's making an effort to be better, he's apologized for how he treated me, and I accepted, and we've moved on.

"Bitchy," Dante answers for him.

I shrug. "Eh, you've not known me long. I can be bitchy when I need to be. Besides, have you met Annemarie?" They all shake their heads, "What about Hayes, Hayden, and Jade?" Again, they shake their heads in the negative. "Well, you're in for a right treat," I say sarcastically, knowing just what arseholes my cousins can be to people they consider as the enemy.

"Right," Makenna comments. "So, she tells Aunt Edwina that she wishes she'd never married Hayes and well, you know our Aunt, she didn't take that lying down."

"Oh my God, what did she do?" I ask with a smile, "Please tell me she hit her."

"Damn, doll face, I never expected you to be so bloodthirsty." Romero smirks at me. As he moves closer to me. Having him this near sends my pulse skyrocketing.

"She didn't hit her, but she told her to keep her mouth shut. She's married now, there's no divorce and if Annemarie wants out, Edwina would be more than willing to assist her. Besides, it's not Edwina that Annemarie should be worried about." Makenna tells us and sighs, we've dealt with women like Annemarie for years, no doubt we'll still continue to deal with them.

"Jade," I say, I miss the crazy girl.

Makenna nods. "When was the last time you spoke to her?"

"A few weeks ago, she was talking about coming out here. But she had to speak to her attorney first."

"Why she got to speak to her attorney?" Dante asks.

"She's on bail at the moment, her court case is in six months' time." I say, "She's being charged with manslaughter." My words come out a little harder than I intended. "Her legal team thinks that because of who her family is, that she'll be doing the maximum term which is about five years."

"Holy shit," Alessio breathes. "Are all the women in your family badass?"

Makenna grins. "Yes. Jade was kidnapped when she was seven, since then her da's made sure that she's able to take care of herself. All of us can fight, we can all shoot a gun, and we can all use a knife."

I nod. "We all know how to drive like a formula one driver. That's something that Da had made sure. He wanted us to be able to get away if need be."

"Wait," Alessio says, "you say we all. Holly, you can fight like Makenna?"

It's Kenna who answers. "Of course she can. She's Danny's sister for fuck sake."

I feel Romero's intense gaze on me, thankfully my phone rings and I take the time to answer it, not wanting to get into this discussion right now.

"Hey Da, what's the craic?" I answer happily, I haven't spoken to him in a few days.

"Hol, I need you to get on the next flight to London," he instructs me.

My gaze collides with Makenna's and she's instantly alert as am I. "What's happened?"

"Fuck," he growls. "Melissa's gone into labor."

"Christ on a bike, Da, it's too early." I gasp, she's only thirty-four weeks pregnant.

"I know, baby girl. Get your arse on a plane. Your brother's no doubt a mess," he tells me.

"Okay, Da, I'll let you know when we're leaving."

"Love you, baby girl."

"Love you too, Da. See you soon." I end the call and see that Makenna's already on hers. "You sorting the flight?" I ask her, trying not to let the panic rise. Melissa and my niece are going to be okay. Lissa is strong as hell and the baby's a Gallagher, we're fierce and determined. We're fighters.

"Yep, we leave in forty-five minutes. Get your shit packed."

I jump down from the counter as does Makenna and I'd smile at the glare that Dante gives her if I weren't so worried about Lissa.

I pray that she and the baby are okay.

WE'RE in our hotel room, and I'm bone tired. I want to collapse on the bed and sleep. Danny and Melissa are okay, as is Annalise. My niece is beautiful and so bloody tiny. But Ma and daughter are doing great and I know Danny's relieved.

"She's okay, doll face," Romero says softly and I stare at him, wondering why he's like this. Why one minute he's mine, he'll do anything for me, and then the next he's barely even my husband.

"I know," I reply, as I look down at my hands, unsure how to even keep my heart safe from him anymore.

"When we return, we'll be moving." He tells me and I glance up at him, we are? "Doll face, you were right what you said to me about moving out of the house and getting our own. Since the day of the shootout in Granny Jones' I've been planning our move. I've purchased a house and it closed this morning. We'll move in once we're back in the States."

I see the determination in his eyes. This is what he wants. "Okay, Rome. Is there anything you need me to do?"

He smiles at me again. "Why am I not surprised that you're not arguing with me."

I raise a brow. "If I argued about it, would it change the outcome?" He shakes his head. "Then what's the point? I'll pick my battles, Rome, and this isn't one of them."

"Now, we need to talk about what happened yesterday." I close my eyes. I knew he wouldn't leave it alone. I knew he'd have to have something to say about it. "You are my wife, Holly, any man touches you, will die."

I sigh. "I didn't do anything, I told him that I'm not interested. It's not my fault."

His eyes flare. "Not your fault? Every fucking morning you go running with him."

I glare at the asshole. "Excuse me? Because I went running and he—by the way—was told to come with me. The things he said..."

Romero's hand closes around my throat as he presses me against the wall. It's not hard or painful, but the pressure is enough for me to know that he's serious. "I heard what he said. That you deserve better than me. He's not wrong. But you're mine. If I find out that you're just like your mom, there's nowhere on this earth you'll be able to hide from me..." he presses his face close to mine, his breath hot against my skin, his hand still tight around my throat. "You're mine, doll face. I'll kill you if you even look at another man."

"I didn't," I say through clenched teeth, pissed that he is accusing me of wrongdoing. "As much as I wish this marriage was different, it's not and there's nothing I can do about it. You're my husband. Til death do us fucking part. Nothing or no one is going to change that. So, take your fucking hand off me."

A glint shines in his eyes. "Mine," he snarls and crashes his lips against mine.

God, I fucking hate how weak I am, how all it takes is one kiss and I'm putty in his hands. Why can't I be stronger and say no?

The truth is so blatantly obvious. I'm in love with my husband. I'm in love with a man that doesn't give a fuck about me. To him, I'm a possession. Someone to own, to dictate to. I'll never be seen as anything else.

EIGHT

ROMERO

TWO MONTHS LATER

We stayed in London for three days. Holly and Makenna wanted to stay and make sure that both Melissa and Annalise were okay before they were comfortable leaving. We went back home and things between Holly and I turned ice cold. We moved out of New York and into our home in Connecticut, but it's as though we're strangers. Hell, since the fucking day of the shootout at Granny Jones's, things between us have been tense. I know that she's pulling away from me. I can feel it. She tries so hard to keep her distance from me during the day, but as soon as night falls, she's riding my cock like she was born to do it.

My wife is an enigma. We've been married for a little over three months and yet, I feel as though I know very little about her. I've come to learn she has an impossible temper, something that the girls claim is to do with them being Irish. I must admit, watching her eyes flash with anger and her nostrils flare when she's pissed is one of the sexiest things I've ever seen and when she unleashes that anger. Fuck me, I'm hard as stone.

Now we're back in London, I swear I spend more fucking time here than home. But this time, I'm needed. Danny was kidnapped, and it turned out that it has to do with the Bratva, which means it has to do with me as those motherfucking Damini's are in bed with them. Kurt, Maruzzo, and Maxim are all still in the wind and it's pissing me off. I need to find them and soon. The longer they're out there, the more Holly's in danger.

My men are on alert, they've finally understood that I'm not someone to mess with. You're either with me or against me and I don't tolerate bullshit. I have no problem offing as many of those that are against me if it gets me to where I want to be. But since the shit with Maruzzo and Maxim, the Irish men have seen me in a different light, they know that I'll do whatever it takes to protect one of their own. My wife.

We're due to leave tomorrow, we've spent time with her family and was here to see Annalise have her baptism. But it's time to go, I need my wife alone. Her family are the biggest cock blockers. Her dad in particular, is constantly calling and checking in on her.

"Doll face?" I call out as I enter the hotel room, I've brought us breakfast.

"Yeah," her voice is distorted behind the closed door to the bathroom. "You okay?"

"Got you some breakfast," I tell her as I set it on the table. She told me it had been a while since she had a full Irish, it took me a while to realize what that was, but luckily the hotel serves it and so I ordered us both one.

My words are met by silence, moments later the bathroom door opens, and the room is filled with steam. "You got me brekkie?"

I roll my eyes at her words, she just can't say the full words, always has to shorten stuff. "Yes, doll face, I got you breakfast. Finish up and come and eat it before it gets cold."

"Hon," she whispers as she walks toward me, her hair damp from the shower and there's not an ounce of makeup on her face. She's dressed in tight black jeans and a black sweater that falls off one of her shoulders. My gaze goes to her feet where she's bare footed.

"What?" I ask, she's got this weird look on her face as though she can't believe that I've got her breakfast.

She sighs as she sits in the chair, bringing her feet up so that her chest is pressed against her knees and she reaches for a sausage. "Growing up, our house was shite. Like ridiculous." She shakes her head as she takes a bite of her food. "Ma would lose her damn mind every time Da would leave the house. She'd constantly accuse him of cheating, even though we all know that she was the one doing that. Even if Da was, I wouldn't blame him, ma's a nightmare."

I pick up the bacon and stare at it in horror. "What the fuck is this?"

She laughs, "That, hon, is a rasher. The shite you have is more like slithers of overcooked fat."

"Mouth," I tell her, and she throws her head back and laughs. She swears more than Makenna. "Carry on with your story, doll face."

Her eyes get soft, and my chest burns at the expression on her face. Fuck. She's digging herself deeper as each day passes. Even when she's angry at me.

"So, as soon as Da would leave, so would Ma, it was left to Danny and Mal to watch over me and Chloe. Mal would do the cooking, he'd always tell me that I needed to eat because I was so damned skinny. He wanted me to put on weight. He'd sit and watch me eat as he knew if he left, I wouldn't finish it. Anyway, he used to say that he'd be only happy if I got married and if the man I married would feed me." She shrugs as though it's not a big deal. "And that's what you're doing." The last words are whispered.

"Why wouldn't you eat?" I ask, she thinks she can just skim over that little fact and I'll leave it alone. Fuck no.

Her eyes narrow at me. "Why do you want to know?" She demands.

I take a calming breath, trying to remind myself not to bristle at her tone. "You're my wife, I want to know everything about you."

She frowns, "You believe you're entitled to know everything? I mean, other than sex, you don't give a fuck about me. I'm just someone you can use as a hole to fill whenever you get the urge."

I'm up off my seat and in her space before she even finishes her sentence. "You think I don't give a fuck about you?" I ask, my voice vibrating with anger. My hands on each side of her hips, as I crowd her.

"Yes," she replies with not an ounce of fear in her face. I'm not sure what to make of that. I don't want my wife to fear me but I'm a fucking monster and nothing is going to change that. "You act as though I'm an imposition, why would I think differently?"

"You're important to me," I say through clenched teeth. "Probably the most important thing."

She blinks and then a beautiful smile forms on her face. "Okay."

Is she for fucking real?

"Pain in my ass," I mutter as I lift her into my arms and

sit down on her seat, pulling her into my lap. "Now fucking talk."

She sighs as she leans back against my chest. Her body curled around mine, fucking perfection. That's what it feels like every time I have her in my arms. "So, Ma is a bitch. You met her at the wedding."

It took everything I had in me not to smack that bitch. The way she spoke about her daughter pissed me off.

"Well, she's always been like that. The first time I remember her telling me that I was fat and needing to stop eating, I was six."

What the fuck?

"It got to me and I used to not eat, until Malcolm realized. I'm okay now, I don't care what she thinks. I'm happy with my body and I love food. She can go fuck herself."

"You're sexy as hell doll face, you have an amazing body, I should know, I worship it every night." I grin at her, loving the giggle that escapes her. "But that doesn't mean that I won't lay your mom out when I see her."

She shakes her head, "She's not worth it. Trust me, Ma isn't worth the hassle, she doesn't get to ruin my life anymore."

I narrow my eyes, there's more that's happened. "What else did she do?"

"I'm not telling you; you'll get angry, and I'll have to deal with the Hulk for the rest of the day."

"Funny, but babe, that's not going to cut it. I want to know what else she did." I hold her closer to me, making sure that she can't escape from the embrace.

"So, there was this guy," I tense at her words, fuck, I didn't expect that. "Calm down Hulk-Man. Nothing happened."

"I know that," I say begrudgingly. I'm not sure how I'll deal with knowing that she had feelings for some other guy.

"Anyway, Da thought it was best if I didn't marry out of obligation. He wanted the best for me and decided that the Mafia life wasn't for me. Or to be submerged in it as I am now. So, I was allowed to date. To say Danny and Mal lost their minds is an understatement. So, I met this guy, Alan." The way she snarls his name makes me smile. She hates him, which means the ass is out of her life. "So, Da wanted to meet him and everything before he took me out on a date." Her body tenses and I wait for her to finish. "Before I invited him, I found him and my Ma together. Ma was already pregnant at the time. So yes, Ma's a bitch and she knew who he was."

"Doll face, he's a dick. Your mom is fake, you are all natural and fucking gorgeous. That dick lost the best thing he ever had and I'm fucking grateful because now you're mine."

Her mom is a fucking bitch. I want nothing more than to be the one to put the fucker down, but I have to get in line, she's pissed off a lot of people.

"No one but Makenna knows about that. If Da found out he'd kill her. I don't want that on my conscience."

"All right, doll face. Enough talk about the bitch. What do you want to do today?"

She reaches for her plate and settles back into me. "I don't mind, I'm not fussy. It'll be nice to spend some time together. I know that when we go home you'll be busy."

She doesn't even realize that she calls America home anymore.

"I can take you sightseeing." I've never done the whole tourist thing, it's not who I am. I don't have the inclination. But for Holly, I'd make an exception.

She waves her sausage in the air. "Hon, you do realise that I'm Irish right?"

I lean forward and take a bite from it. "Yeah, and?" I say with a mouthful of food.

She rolls her eyes. "I mean, it's like a hop, skip, and jump across the pond. I don't need you to take me sightseeing. We used to come a couple of times a year. More even. I can show you some good spots, places that won't be crawling with tourists, if you want?"

Do I want to spend the day trailing around London? Fuck no. Do I want to spend the day with my wife? Hell fucking yes. "All right, doll face, you show me the cool spots."

She giggles. "You know that you're not down with the kids, right?"

"Babe...."

She rests her head against my shoulder. "You're all right, you know?"

I raise a brow. "Just all right?"

She nods, her lips pursed. "Yep, in bed, you're amazing." She rolls her eyes. "Don't let it get to your head, Rome, it's big enough as it is."

"So, I'm just all right, as you would say, in other aspects."

"You're an arse, I didn't mean it in a bad way. I only meant that from what I had heard about you, you're actually sweet."

I scowl. Sweet? "Doll face, did you have the shower set to hot? Are you dehydrated?"

"No, now shut up and let me finish my breakfast. I won't say another word."

I kiss her neck, letting her know that I'm not angry, in fact, I'm far from it. This is the most relaxed I've seen her.

"By the way," she says after a few minutes of silence. "I love our house."

I smile into her hair as I press a kiss against it. It was the house that she was looking at. I saw it one day while she left her laptop open. She'd been looking at houses in case we were to move to Connecticut. So as soon as I saw it, I knew I had to get it.

"It was the one you wanted."

She glances up at me. "Yeah, hon, it was. You're sneaky, you know that?"

I wink at her and I'm rewarded with her soft smile. "Only when I need to be." I pull her up so that she's straddling me. I need to be inside of her.

No matter what, I just can't get enough of her.

NINE
HOLLY

"Doll face," Romero says as he strolls into my office and closes the door behind him. "You almost finished?"

I glance up at him, he's in a crisp white shirt, his suit jacket folded over his arm. He looks hot, and I'm glad that I bought my dress. It's black, tight, and I feel sexy as hell in it. My hair is curled and falls down my back. I'm wearing heels that I know I'll end up paying for tomorrow. When Makenna and I went shopping for this party that's happening tonight I knew immediately this dress was the one for me. It's tight across my breasts, cinches in at my waist and hits mid-thigh. It's not something I'd usually wear.

"Just a sec," I tell him and hit send on the email that I was typing up for Granda. Once the email is sent, I shut down the computer and get to my feet. "All done, are you okay?"

He frowns at me as he moves toward me. "Of course. Why wouldn't I be?" He's lying, I may have only been married to him for a short while, but I know when he's lying to me. His lips thin, I must give it to him though, it's a slight tell and only someone who knows him will see it.

"Because you're home, it's not even lunch time yet." I tell him, I rarely see him before six every evening. Even then, that's the rare occasion. It's more like eight or nine at night before he walks in the door and even then, he goes to his office and spends another few hours there. Not to mention, he said he'd meet me at his cousin's house this evening.

"Can I not come home to see my wife?" he says as he pulls me into his arms.

"I suppose," I mutter as my hands go around his waist. Things between us have gotten better, he's not as closed off anymore. When we're together it's perfect. He's perfect. Attentive, sweet, and caring. When we're not alone, he's closed off. I get it, I don't like it, but I get it. He's the Underboss, he needs to not show weakness. "Did you find them yet?"

His body tenses beneath my hands. "What?" His voice is harsh.

"Look, Rome, I'm not stupid or naive. I know that something is going on and that it has to do with the Damini's. You've upped the security around the house, and I'm not allowed to leave without at least two men on me and that's not including you. So, I won't ask other than have you found them yet?"

His arms tighten around me, practically crushing me. "No, doll face, I haven't."

I sigh resting my head against his chest. "I've tried to chase their money, but they haven't touched their accounts."

"Doll face, I get that you want to help, but no more. You've already got a target on your back."

My breath hitches at his words. God, I fucking knew it. "But, Rome, that gives me even more reason to do it. They already want me dead."

"Don't fucking say that shit," he growls. "That's not going to happen."

I tilt my head so that I can look at his face. "I know, are you ready to go?" I ask. He's all dressed up ready for the party, that has to be why he's home early.

He shakes his head. "No, nowhere fucking near," he says as he captures my lips. "You look so fucking sexy," he says, his voice hoarse and thick with lust. "I'm rock hard." He grinds his cock against me, and I bite back a whimper.

"Rome," I sigh, "we don't have time."

He nips at my lip. "Don't care. I'm not leaving this office until I fuck you. Until my cum is leaking out of you. If I have to be in a room full of assholes that are going to be staring at you, they'll damn well know who you belong to."

Why the hell do I find that such a turn on? Anytime Rome stakes his claim I'm like putty in his hands. "A quickie," I tell him as I deepen the kiss.

His hands skim my thighs, he pushes the hem of my dress up to my waist. "Never had a quickie with you, doll face, anytime my cock hits your pussy, you fuck me like a porn star. You think that I'm rushing that?" He shakes his head as he smirks at me. "Babe, watching you come apart is the fucking best thing about my day."

"Rome," I whisper, wiggling against him.

"Bend over your desk, doll face."

I do exactly as he orders, my hands flat against my desk, my arse up in the air, my dress hiked up around my waist. I'm soaked, as I am anytime Rome talks dirty to me, or even touches me. He's lethal and I'm irrevocably in love with the man.

His hand caresses my arse and I wiggle beneath his touch. Needing more, when he removes his hand, I whine only to hear his chuckle. "Ro..." My words are cut off by my gasp as his hand comes down onto my arse hard.

"That," he says thickly, "is for wearing this motherfucking dress." He lifts off his hand again and brings it down once more. The sound of his palm hitting my flesh fills the room. "That is for driving me crazy. I'm going to be hard all fucking night."

I can't help it, I push back against him, urging him to continue.

He freezes. "You like that doll face."

"Please," I beg. I know that I'm safe with Rome. Whatever I want in bed, he gives it to me.

"Fuck," he growls and this time when his palm connects with my arse cheek I moan and push back again. "Perfect, fucking perfect."

He's driving me wild, I'm so close to coming. "Rome, please."

He pushes aside my panties and thrusts into me. He's so thick, his movements make me sore. But a good sore. So, fucking good, I'm mewling like a bloody cat, begging for more. Harder, faster, anything to push me over the edge.

"Told you, doll face, you fuck me like you were born to do it," he pants as his fingers dig into my arse. He's an arse man, always has his eyes on mine.

"Rome, please, I need more." He treats me as though I'm fragile. As though I'm a delicate doll that's going to break if he lets go.

"Fuck," he says through clenched teeth.

I move slightly, my hand reaching down between my legs where his cock is pounding into my pussy. My fingers touch his balls and the hiss he releases tells me that he's close to the edge. Well, it's time to send him over. I cup them, rolling them in my hand and I bite my lip when he thrusts into me and stills.

"Doll face, move your hand."

I shake my head. "Not happening, now fuck me."

"I don't want to hurt you," he says and I've had enough. I use all my strength and push him off me. "Hol?"

I spin around, my ass on the desk as I glare at my husband. "If it were me that was holding back from you, you'd lose your damn mind. I want my husband, Romero. All of him. I am not a fragile doll, no matter what you think."

His hands grip my thighs, and he pulls me toward him, my back hitting the desk as he impales me on his cock. "To you, I am not a monster. I don't want that to change."

My hand goes to his face, his brown eyes filled with worry. "Rome," I whisper as he slowly thrusts into me. "You think I don't know who you are. Or what you're capable of? You are a monster. To everyone out there. In here, in our house, to me, you're Rome. My Rome. My husband. So, please, don't ever think that I'll think of you as anything but the man I love. Now fuck me like you mean it."

I see the moment that the last ounce of restraint goes. Those beautiful brown eyes of his practically turn black. His hands go to my hips and the grip is painful and I know that they'll leave a bruise, his thrusts are fast, brutal, and perfect.

I move so that my arms are wrapped around his neck, my lips against his face. I need to be close to him, I need to have this connection to him. I'm fucking him back with just as much abandonment, lust, and want. We're both groaning and moaning so loudly, neither of us care if anyone's listening.

His teeth are nipping at my neck, he's marking me, making a statement of ownership.

I'm whimpering with each thrust; my orgasm has been building for so long. I need to cum. My body shakes with need. I'm gasping trying to reach for the ultimate high.

"Rome," I beg.

"Not yet, doll face," he grunts as he thrusts harder and faster.

I throw myself back, needing something to keep myself up. My back hits the desk as my body tightens.

"Do not fucking come," he snarls.

"Please!" I'm reduced to a whimpering mess. "Rome, God, please, hon."

"Now," he grounds out as he thrusts hard into me, rooting himself to the hilt. "Fuck, Hol, come now."

I do, and my body spasms as I detonate, his name a cry from my lips.

Crashing sounds around us, but I ignore it, my gaze fixated on Rome as his body shudders while he comes inside of me.

He collapses back onto the chair and he pulls me down on top of him. His face buried into my neck.

"That was amazing," I say as I manage to catch my breath.

He raises his head, his eyes gazing around the room, his body starts to shake and I'm instantly worried, that is until I realise that he's laughing. "Doll face. I'm going to have to buy you a new computer."

My eyes widen at the smile on his face, and I turn to see the destruction that was once my office. My computer is lying on the floor, the screen smashed to pieces, all the paperwork that was on my desk is now scattered on the ground.

I shrug. "Eh, it was so fucking worth it."

His eyes soften. "Hol," his voice sounds a little weird and I know that he's worried he's hurt me.

"That was the sexiest thing I've ever seen. The way you lost control..." I shake my head. "Please don't go back to treating me like I'm breakable. I want all of you Rome, every single piece of you."

His lips touch mine and I sink against him. Nothing is better than being held by him.

"We have to get ready," I tell him, hating that we have to move from this position.

"Yeah, we won't stay too long, just enough to make our presence known."

I laugh, "Hon, that'll happen from the moment we walk in. You're an imposing sight. You never smile, you either stare at people or glare at them."

"That's not true," he says as his arms tighten around me. "I smile with you."

My heart soars at his words. It's true, he does smile when he's alone with me. He places a soft kiss against my forehead, and I close my eyes and savor the feeling. God, I really love this man.

"You ready, doll face?"

I nod. "As I'll ever be. I need to freshen up." I tell him as I get up off his lap. "Can you tidy up a little?" I ask as I bite my lip and glance around the room.

He stands up behind me, his hand going to my hip. "I've got it, Hol, go do whatever you need to, then we'll leave."

I give him a soft smile and walk toward the door. I need to find a bathroom and get cleaned up. Once I'm behind the safety of the locked bathroom door, I realise that I told him that I loved him and I got nothing in return. It hurts. Fucking stings. Tears well in my eyes.

Then his words run through my mind.

"You're important to me."

"Probably the most important thing."

"I smile with you."

He may not love me, but he shows me how much he cares about me. This isn't like my parents' marriage; this is far from it. My husband cares about me and I love him.

That's good enough for me. I can love a man that doesn't love me but cares deeply for me.

TEN
ROMERO

"A little heads up, Rome," Dante begins as Holly and I walk toward him. "Georgina is here."

Holly tenses beside me. Fucking Georgina. What the fuck is she doing here?

"Who invited that viper?" Alessio asks and I see the way he's glancing at Holly, he's worried about her. Georgina is the type of woman that will use any weakness against you. Since we had words about his behavior toward my wife, he's changed. He's finally seen the error of his ways. Finally owning up and becoming the man I knew him to be.

"Fuck knows," Dante says, "Makenna's on the warpath. She's ready to tear her head off."

My hand moves to Holly's waist and I pull her into my side. "Doll face?" I murmur.

My brothers moved away giving us some privacy.

"Have you spoken to her since the wedding?" She asks me, her voice void of emotion. I fucking hate that I can't tell what she's thinking.

"No, I haven't. I wouldn't do that to you." I'm pissed that she even asked me that shit.

"Rome," she says softly, "this is all new to me. Loving someone isn't easy, especially you. I'm not like her; I don't know how to play the stupid games she plays. Okay?"

Fuck. She's so open and honest. "Holly, no one," I say so that only she can hear me, my grip on her hip tightening, I pull her into me. Not giving a fuck who sees us right now. "No one but you has ever said that to me."

She tilts her head, as though she's studying me. "Said what?"

Fuck.

"That they love me," I tell her honestly.

She blinks furiously, as though she's trying to stop herself from crying. "I do," she says fiercely. "I love you so much that it hurts. I hate that you've never felt love before. I despise your family, Rome. Even my brothers love me, and they let me know it. I don't give a fuck if you're men. That's no excuse."

"Babe..."

She shakes her head, "No. Listen, please," her pleading is something I can't ignore. "I get it, Rome, you're not able to love me and while it's shit, it hurts, I also know that you care a fucking lot about me and that's more than enough for me. But I'm going to love you. I'm always going to. No one can stop me. So, *please*, don't hurt me."

I rest my forehead against hers wondering how the fuck I got so lucky to have someone so fucking pure to be in my life.

"You've not spoken to her and I trust you. So, let's go in there, make an appearance and then we can go home. Because I'm going to want to have a replay of what happened in my office," she says with a grin.

I'm not sure what love is. If I were capable of it, I'd love Holly in a fucking heartbeat. She's the only woman in this world who gets all of me. Every single fucking piece of me. I wouldn't have it any other way.

"Keep talking and we won't make it home before we do a replay."

A slow grin forms on her face. "Do you think there's an office here?"

I can't stop the chuckle that spills from my lips, her eyes once again soften. "I need to make you do that more often."

"I'm close to fucking you right here, doll face."

Her cheeks heat and I know that she wants me. God, this woman is made for me.

"Holly," Makenna's voice calls out and I step back, the disappointment in my wife's eyes hits my gut. "God, that woman is such a fucking bitch."

Holly raises a brow. "Who?"

"Georgina, she's been asking for Romero." Makenna glares at me as though this is my fault. "She thinks that he's going to see her and then he'll be in her bed. Again."

Holly giggles and I raise a brow. "I don't find this funny."

"Hon, she's desperate. You were a man whore, but you don't do desperate."

"I was not a man whore." I gripe and she gives me a knowing smirk.

"You were, don't lie. You've got to remember, Hon, that I was told every story about you. How you were the ladies' man and a monster."

"Who the fuck told you that?" I ask, wanting to find them and kill them.

"My brothers."

Well fuck.

"Rome, you're not that man with me. Surely you see that." She tells me as she links her arm through mine.

"You're the man that I love," she tells me softly so that only I can hear her.

"You gonna keep saying that to me, aren't you?"

She gives me a look that says what do you think.

"Are we going to stand out here all evening?" Alessio asks. The impatient fuck.

I ignore him and walk toward the entrance of the mansion.

"Jesus," Holly mutters, "did she forget to put on clothes?"

Dante chuckles. "I love this bitchy side to Holly."

"I think she's being rather tame. If it were me and your ex did what Georgina's doing, I'd have killed her by now."

Holly grins, "I can control my temper, Kenna. Besides, nothing gets to bitches like her than being ignored. Although, the way Ales's eyes are practically popping out of his head, I doubt we'll all be ignoring her." The disgust in her voice makes me glare at Alessio.

"Hol, she's got nothing on you. Trust me," my brother says not realizing how close to death he really is.

"Romero," Georgina purrs as she walks over to us. An ugly smile on her face and I can't help but think what the fuck I ever saw in her. Then again, the way she has no gag reflex helped a lot. She lifts her hand as if to touch me and Holly's fingers close around her wrist. It must be a tight grip because pain flashes through Georgina's eyes. "Jealous," she sneers at my wife.

Holly laughs. "No, but you are. You do not touch him. You seriously can't be this desperate, Georgia."

Georgina narrows her eyes, her lips thinning. "It's Georgina," she stamps her foot.

Holly shakes her head, "Same thing. Now, why don't you run along before I lose my temper."

She shrieks. "You fucking bitch." She sneers at my wife.

I take a step toward her. "What the fuck did I tell you?" I snarl at her, my words filled with anger and she flinches. Good. "You do not talk to my wife like that. Fuck. You don't even look at her. Stay the fuck away from us, Georgina."

Tears fill her eyes. "But we were so good together," she whispers as though that's meant to mean anything.

"You were good on your knees, Georgina. That's all. Ask any man in here, the majority have had you. Do you think any man wants someone like you? Not one of them is even paying you any attention. Take a look," I tell her and smirk as she glances around. Every man's eyes are on my fucking wife. "You are not even in the same league as her. This is the last warning you get. You come near her again and I'm going to forget that you're a woman and snap your fucking neck."

Her eyes are wide, and she glances toward Holly.

"Don't fucking look at her," I snarl at her. Beyond fucking pissed that she's trying to ruin my marriage. The one thing that I hold above all else.

I smirk at her as I watch Carter storm toward us. "What the fuck did I say to you, Georgina?" His voice low, the anger coming off him in waves. "You do not fuck with me." He grabs her arm and pulls her toward him.

"Dad," an unknown voice calls out and I watch as Carter blanches. The anger disappears instantly as he turns to the blonde girl, she's young. Too fucking young to be at this party. "Mom's looking for *her*," the way she spits the word her, tells me that we're not the only ones that Georgina has pissed off, this girl is glaring at her with hatred.

"Okay, Destiny, I'll be there in a second. I need to sort this mess out," he tells the girl, his focus still on Georgina.

Fucking hell, how the hell has Carter managed to keep his daughter out of the spotlight for so long? I haven't seen that girl since she was six.

Destiny glares at Georgina. "Aren't you sick of sorting her shit out? You should have sent her to boarding school."

I hear the sharp intake of breath from Holly and see that she's trying to stop the laughter.

"You always were a fucking bitch, Dest," Georgina says and I have to admit, the woman's got balls, especially to say that in front of Carter.

"Better to be a bitch than a desperate whore," Destiny fires back. "We all saw them, George, fuck, it was like foreplay. You think you're going to come between them." Destiny shakes her head. "I knew you were stupid, I didn't think you had a death wish."

"What would you know? You're a frigid bitch."

Destiny laughs. "No, I have some self-respect." She glances at her father. "I take it we have to leave now?"

Carter sighs. "Yeah, we're leaving."

Destiny glares at Georgina. "Great, thank fuck I'm leaving tomorrow." She turns and walks away.

"I like her," Holly announces.

"Same," Makenna replies. "She has taste. How old is she?"

Carter sighs yet again, not once letting go of Georgina. "Seventeen going on twenty." He leans down and whispers something into Georgina's ear which makes her tense. She nods and walks away.

"I apologize for my niece," he says and I'm wondering when he's going to realize enough is e-fucking-enough. His brother died and the viper went to live with him. Obviously, she's a fucking bitch to everyone, even his daughter hates him. "She'll not cause you and your wife any more trouble. I assure you."

"I'll hold you to that," I tell him and watch him bristle.

"She does or says one more thing, I'm holding you personally responsible."

He glares at me before walking off.

"Well, that was an interesting start to the evening," Holly says. "All that was missing was the popcorn. I need a drink."

"I hate you," Makenna grumbles. "I want a drink, too."

Holly steps closer to her, a weak smile on her face. "I'll get you some tea."

"God, you're evil." Makenna groans, "Where's Antonio?" She asks, glancing around the mansion. He's a cousin of ours and this is his party. The fucking asshole. He's flashy as hell.

"Knowing, Antonio, he's already found a woman for the evening," Alessio comments and both women shake their heads in disgust.

I pull Holly into my body. "We need to find an empty room."

Her eyes dilate. "Rome," she whispers, and I smirk; she's fucking perfect for me.

I pull her with me as we go in search of an empty room. I need to be inside her.

"DO you want to come home with us? I have your room all ready for you," Makenna says as we step out of Antonio's house.

Holly shivers and I take my suit jacket off and wrap it around her. She gives me her soft smile, the one that hits me in the gut. "What do you want to do, doll face?"

She rests her head against my chest. "I'm tired, if we

drive home, I'll probably be asleep before we even leave the state. You're the one that's driving, it's up to you."

"We'll stay tonight," I tell them as I wrap my arm around Holly's shoulder and move her toward my car. "Meet you back at the house."

Dante gives me a chin lift as he leads Makenna to the waiting car.

"You doing okay, doll face?" I ask her, she's been tired a lot lately.

"Yeah, I think I'm overdoing it. With the move, all the travelling between here and London. It's catching up with me."

"You do too much." She works hard, and sometimes I'll find her in bed, her laptop beside her and she's fast asleep.

She raises a brow. "Oh, I'm sorry, pot, meet kettle."

Tires squeal and I glance around just in time to see a car speeding toward me. It's as though time slows down, and the car advances on us. The man on the passenger's side has a gun pointed at us. I reach to push Holly to the ground, to get her the fuck out of the way. But instead, her delicate hands are at my chest, pushing as hard as she can.

I hit the ground with a thud as a gunshot rings out. My world stops when I hear Holly's painful cry and she crumbles to the ground.

ELEVEN
ROMERO

I push to my feet, my breathing hard. "Doll face!" I'm over to her in seconds. My heart stutters with every step I take.

Fuck. Is that my voice? It's shaky.

I drop to my knees beside her, her head's bleeding profusely. "Baby?" I whisper, unable to believe that this is fucking happening. Her eyes are closed, her usually creamy skin is pale and gray. My fingers go to her neck and I want to weep with relief when I feel the thumping of her pulse beneath my touch.

I fucked up. I've never reacted that slowly before. I'm her husband. I'm supposed to protect her. That's my job. I'm the one that's meant to keep her safe, I'm supposed to keep the worst of this life away from her. I failed her. Now she's lying on the ground, blood pouring from her face and all I can think of is that I could lose her. That the one person I care about above all else, could have fucking died.

Someone is going to pay. I will not stop until whoever the fuck did this is six feet under.

Tires screech again, my hand goes to the gun that I have holstered at my back. My gaze scanning the cars that are parked. Then I see Dante's car squealing to a stop. Makenna rushes out of the vehicle and over to us.

"What the hell happened?" she asks as she starts to look over Holly, her gaze firmly on my wife. "Fuck, we need to stop this bleeding. Fucking head wounds," she mutters.

"We need to get her back to the house," Stefan says, he's Dante and Makenna's security team, he grew up with Dante and I, his father was part of the famiglia just as ours was. "It's too open out here."

I lift Holly into my arms, not once does she stir. My gut tightens as I run toward my car. "Why the fuck isn't she awake?" I growl as Makenna crawls into the back seat with me.

"I don't know, I really don't," she says and I know that she's having a hard time just as I am. This is her niece.

Dante jumps into the passenger's seat as Stefan slides into the driver's seat. The rest of their team will follow behind us. Stefan puts his foot down and gets us the hell out of this fucking place. It shouldn't take us too long to get to the house. The sooner the fucking better.

"This shouldn't have happened." I can't stop staring at my wife's lifeless form. God, never again. I'm tying her ass to the bed, she's not allowed to leave the house.

"No," Makenna snaps, "it fucking shouldn't. How the hell did she get shot?"

I glare at the woman who I have come to respect, that is not only family, but the boss, and I don't give a fuck if she can see the anger and darkness that's swirling in my eyes. I'm so close to the edge right now, I'm holding on by a thread.

"She fucking pushed me out of the way." I say through clenched teeth, fuck. I can't believe that she did that. What the hell was she thinking?

"That's our Holly," she murmurs and the use of *ours* pisses me off. Holly is mine. "When she loves, she loves hard. She'd have been devastated if you had been the one that was shot."

"She shouldn't have fucking done it!" I snap, pissed that she'd endanger her life for mine. She's innocent, pure, perfect.

This is my way of life. The bullets are part of my world. The death and destruction come hand in hand. I'm so deep that I fucking bleed this life. Holly, she shouldn't even be tainted with it.

"Do we know who did it yet?" I ask, needing to have information on this.

"Adriano, Bosco, and Franco are tailing them. They'll have back up soon enough," Dante assures me. "Whoever the fuck did this is going to pay."

Too fucking right, they will. "They're mine."

No one else touches them. I own that right. They shot my fucking wife. They made her bleed. I'll repay the favor in kind. Those motherfuckers are going to be screaming for mercy when I'm finished with them.

I don't offer mercy. I never have. But this time is different, I feel it deep in my bones. The anger I have is unlike anything I've experienced and it's because of who they targeted. My one savior. My wife.

As soon as Stefan pulls into the drive of the house, I'm moving. The bleeding hasn't stopped, and she hasn't moved an inch. Makenna walks ahead of me, bringing us to the room that not that fucking long ago, Alessio was bleeding out in. I lay Holly on the table and stay close while Makenna gets to work.

She moves effortlessly as she cleans the wound, her shoulder slump forward in relief, "It's only a graze, head wounds bleed a lot. She's got a goose egg at the back of her head, probably where she went down. She's going to be okay."

I nod, unable to speak right now. I'm so fucking close to the edge, the anger bubbling to the surface. "Romero," Dante says and I slice my gaze to him. "They got them," he says, and I smirk. Fuck yes. "Two Bratva bastards," he spits the words out, like they leave a bad taste in his mouth. "The men are bringing them in."

"Thanks." My voice is darker than I've heard in a long time.

"She's going to need to be checked on every hour," Makenna announces, cutting through the silence. "While you're gone, I'll stay with her." She glances around. "Where's Alessio?"

I lift Holly from the bed, "I don't know, I'm going to bring her to our room."

Makenna's gaze is soft as she looks at my unconscious wife lying in my arms. "I'll come and check on her soon."

I don't answer her, I walk out of the room and down the hall. Each step I take is heavy on my heart. This is my fucking fault. The fucking Bratva. My father and his shit. The sins of my father are coming for us and Holly's had to pay.

No more.

Tonight, I'm sending a message.

You do not fuck with my wife.

She's off limits to everyone.

I'll go to fucking war to protect her.

When we reach our bedroom, I push the door open and lay her down on the bed. Blood soaks her hair and face. Seeing it is a knife to the chest. I grab a washcloth from the bathroom and begin to clean her face. I need to get the blood off her face, I need her to be clean.

I knew that Holly meant something to me. Knew it from the get go. Those soft smiles she has that belong to me and me alone, not to mention the way she seeks me out in bed. She may be angry at me, but at night, after she falls asleep she pins me to the bed, her leg entwined with mine and her head on my chest. It's the fucking best feeling in the world. Knowing that even though she's fucking pissed, she still wants me, still trusts me.

Holly is the only person in this world that will ever have my trust. She's the one that I know will never use it against me or hurt me. Before her, I never wanted attachments, I didn't want the responsibility of having to be a husband. I perceived marriage as a hardship, that it would be something that would take a great deal of effort and time. Things I didn't have to give. But as soon as I got to know Holly, all those perceptions went away. I relish the time that I spend with her. I keep her away from the spotlight as I don't want her to be a target. Yet, that's exactly what's happened.

She begins to stir and I'm right there, holding her hand.

"Rome," she whispers as she glances around the room, her hand tightening in mine. "Rome?"

"Right here, doll face," I tell her as I lean over her.

That soft smile is like a balm to the anger that I have rolling through my body. She's awake. That's all that fucking matters right now. I push all the anger aside and focus on her.

"You're okay," she says, her gaze roaming my face.

"Yeah, baby, I'm okay. Although your ass is going to be red by the time I'm finished with you." I push my face closer to hers, my mouth hovering just above hers.

"I'm not sorry," she replies, her mouth set into a harsh

line. "I love you, Rome, I can't and won't let anything happen to you."

"You are my wife," I growl, needing her to realize how much she's fucked up. "You are my fucking life, Holly." Her eyes widen at my words. "You do not push me out of the fucking way. You do not put yourself in danger for me. And you sure as shit do not fucking get shot."

Tears fall from her eyes and I feel like a bastard. "I'm sorry, I didn't mean to get shot, I moved too slowly."

I pull her into my arms. "Never again."

She nods. "Never again." Her promise settles something deep inside. "I'm sorry I scared you."

I shake my head, "Scared me? Fuck doll face. I thought you were fucking dead." That's something that I'll never get out of my mind. The painful cry followed by silence. Fuck.

She cries harder, her hands clawing at my chest. "I'm sorry, God, I can't imagine that. I hurt just thinking about it happening to you."

I kiss her head; this conversation needs to end. "It's over, you're okay. You're here," I tell her and she nods against me. "I'm going to go out soon. Makenna will be here to keep an eye on you. You were unconscious for a while. You've got a concussion from where you fell."

She tenses beneath me. "Where are you going?"

"Doll face, you think I'm going to sit back and let those bastards who shot you get away with it?"

She leans back and looks up at me, her eyes filled with tears, but I see the hope shining in them. "You found them?"

I nod, "Yeah, they're not going to get a chance to do this shit again." I hold her tighter against me. "You're safe."

Her hand rests against my cheek, fuck, this woman knows how to disarm me. "I trust you Rome, I know that you'll do whatever it takes to keep me safe. I love you so much," she says as the tears continue to fall. "Please come home to me in one piece."

I smile, damn, I can't remember the last time someone was worried about me. Fuck. If there's ever been anyone worried about me before. Not the way that Holly does. "No one or nothing can stop me coming home to you."

She yawns and I know that she's going to want to sleep again. "Rest, doll face. Makenna will be here soon to check on you."

I kiss her lips softly once I have her tucked into bed. Her eyes closed as she sinks into the bed. "I'll be home later."

She nods, not once opening her eyes, "Be safe," she whispers to me.

I turn away from her. Seeing her lying on the bed, so fragile and vulnerable is pulling at all my protective instincts to stay with her. To make sure that she's okay.

But I need to do this. I need to make the message clear. Holly is off fucking limits.

"Ready?" Dante asks as soon as I close the door to our bedroom.

I give him a look, one that says, 'what the fuck do you think?'

"She woke up and remembers what happened," I tell Makenna. "She's asleep again."

Makenna nods, relief shining brightly in her eyes. "Okay, I'll go and sit with her."

I give her a chin lift and make my way out of the house.

"I'm going to go out on a limb," Stefan says as I slide into the car, "and say, that these two assholes we have are going to be in a world of pain when you're finished with them."

I shake my head. "No, they'll be dead."

TWELVE

HOLLY

The door opens and I think that it's Romero coming back, that is until I smell Makenna's perfume. Floral and fresh.

"You're awake," she observes as she climbs onto the bed.

I nod. "Yeah, I knew that if Rome knew I was awake he'd have stayed and right now, he needs to be doing what he does best. Stopping these bastards."

She nods. "I've never seen him like that before. I've always known that Romero was dangerous, that his darkness is worse than Dante's. But I never saw it lurking that close to the edge before."

I let out a breath, I'm so worried about him. I know that this is his job. It's who he is, but I can't stop thinking about what could happen.

"He cares about you, Hol, I never thought I'd see him in love."

I blink, "He's not in love. He doesn't do love, he's told me that more than enough, I don't know what happened to him, I'm not sure I'll ever know, but whatever it was, it made him the man he is."

"Holly, that man loves you."

I shake my head. "No, he doesn't. He cares about me, a hell of a lot. But he doesn't love me."

No matter how much I want to hear those three words, I know that I never will. Not from Romero and that's okay. It hurts telling him that I love him and not have the words repeated back. But this is the life I agreed too. There's nothing that I can do about it. I have to grin and bear it.

"How are you feeling?" she asks, changing the subject.

"I've got a headache, I'm sore, and I'm tired. But I'm okay. I know that it could have been a hell of a lot worse." My head is pounding, the pain has slowly started to move into my right eye.

"I'll get you some pain killers. Why don't you call your da? He'll want to know, and he'll be pissed if he finds out from someone else."

I sigh, she's right. But knowing Da, he'll be on the plane within an hour, making a quick pit stop to London to get Danny before flying out here.

"You call him, I'll be back in a while, I'll order some food for us. Neither of us is going to sleep until Dante and Romero are home." She climbs off the bed and leaves the room.

There's no way I can sleep, my stomach is in knots, I'm waiting for the phone to ring or for him to walk through the door. I've never felt this worry before. I wanted him to stay with me, I'm scared, but I know that Rome needed to do whatever he had to end this. I know what this life is, how cruel and unforgiving it can be. My entire family is wrapped so tightly in this world that we bleed mafia. My Da's the head of the Mafia in Ireland, his Da the head of New York. Makenna the head of the East Coast. Her brothers are all Underbosses, and then there's my brothers.

Danny, the eldest, is the head of the UK and Malcolm is the head of Spain.

Malcom's the reason that both Danny and Da are able to be the biggest drug suppliers in Europe. Mal's able to get the drugs out of Spain and smuggle them in trucks. I've seen them concealed in all sorts of shipments, from medical equipment, to clothes, to fucking toys. The trucker will drive from Spain and into France before driving into the UK and into the countryside where they'll deposit the drugs for Danny and for Da, the trucker won't stop once they hit the UK until they hit Wales, from there they'll take the ferry to Dublin.

It's a lucrative business, one that Malcolm has made a profit from. He's richer than all of my family members. He's in the heart of Spain, where all the tourists are, he's not only the Kingpin, he's also a very successful hotelier and nightclub owner.

I reach for my phone and smile when I see that it's charging. I wonder when Rome did that? I hit my da's number and listen to it ring. It's late here, almost eleven in the evening which means it's almost four in the morning in Ireland.

"BABY GIRL WHAT'S HAPPENED?" His voice is tight and alert. There's no hint of sleep at all.

"I'M OKAY," I tell him, needing to reassure him of that right off the bat. "There was a little trouble at the party we went to this evening. Someone tried to shoot Romero and I pushed him out of the way."

. . .

I'M HOPING that ripping off the Band-Aid and telling him quickly will help ease the worry he'll have.

"I WAS GRAZED BY THE BULLET."

I HEAR his sharp intake of breath. "You were what?"

"DA, I'm fine. I promise. It was just a graze. I'm at Makenna's house."

"WHERE'S ROMERO?" he demands, I can hear movement and I know that he's getting ready to leave. He'll be here tomorrow.

"DADDY," I whisper, I haven't called him that in a long time. "I'm okay," I assure him once again. "Rome's gone. They have who did this."

"RIGHT, baby girl. I'll call you back in a while. I've got a few things to organize first. Now, are you sure you're okay? This isn't when you told me that you had a tummy ache and you were fine when in fact your appendix was about ready to burst?"

I WANT to laugh but know that he'll not take too kindly to that. Instead, I smile. "I promise I have a slight headache from where I smashed my head off the ground. But I'm okay."

"OKAY, I'll call you in a couple of hours," he tells me and I hear the tightness in his voice.

"Da, you don't have to come here."

"Holly Jane Gallagher, You've been shot, where the fuck do you think I'm going to go? You are my daughter. I'll be there later today."

Damn, it was worth a try. "Okay, but Da, don't go calling Danny."

"I'll talk to you later. Love you," he says and before I can return the sentiment, he hangs up on me.

I also noticed he didn't say he wouldn't tell Danny. Damn it. I'm going to have two very angry men trying to boss me around when they get here. Not to mention having Makenna hovering over me and then there's Rome, I have no idea how he's going to take this. He could go one of two ways, he can push me away which will kill me or he'll become overbearing like Da and Danny are going to be.

I throw my phone onto the bed beside me and curl up into a ball. My mind racing with what Romero may be doing, if he's being hurt or not. But my ultimate fear is that he'll let his darkness consume him and I'll not be able to pull him back from it.

The door opens once again and Makenna strolls in, she's got pop tarts in her hands and a glass of water. "Let me guess," she begins as she climbs onto the bed beside me. "Denis is coming."

I nod. "I told him not to come and he ignored me. I'd say Danny and Melissa will be here too."

Makenna smiles "Not that you're complaining, you get to see Annalise."

I miss my niece, it's the worst thing about not being in Ireland. I don't get to see my family as much as I used too. Whenever I missed my brothers I'd get on a plane and go visit them. Usually Da would come with me. As much as he pretends that he's okay, he hates being around Ma, I don't blame him. She's flaunted her infidelity in his face for years. I'm not sure what she has over him, but whatever it is has to be huge. Otherwise he'd have killed her by now. He's killed for less.

The pain in my head starts to get worse, I close my eyes hoping that it'll help.

"Take a pill first, Hol. It could help with the pain in your head," Makenna says softly.

I open my eyes and see her holding out a couple of pills for me. I take them and sigh, "I hope it goes away. Fucking thing is moving into my eye."

"I've seen the goose egg on your head. You must have whacked your head hard against the ground. I'm not surprised you've got a killer headache. Once we've eaten, please try and get some sleep."

I nod. "I will, I promise."

She flashes me a grin, "So, now that we're alone, how are things going with you and Romero?"

Butterflies hit my stomach, as they do anytime I think of how happy I am with my husband.

"Good," I tell her with a smile. "I know we don't have the marriage that you and Dante have or what Danny has with Lissa, but I'm happy and he shows me every day that he cares about me." I shrug, not sure what else to say. "It works for us."

She nods. "You both are happy. He's very cautious about

letting people see how happy he is. He's always on alert, even around Dante and I." She clenches her jaw, I know that pisses her off, I can't say that I fully understand why he does it. But he wants to protect me. "But, I see the subtle changes in him."

"He's different from his brother's. He's more intense, I'm not sure what the fuck that arsehole Matteo did to him, but I'm glad that he's dead. I hate that man," I say through clenched teeth.

Matteo Bianchi was a first-class wanker. He hurt Makenna when she was fourteen. He and her Ma were having an affair, and Makenna overheard them. Matteo demanded that her Ma kill her and the bitch tried. She almost killed her own daughter to keep her filthy secret. Years later, Matteo thought he'd fuck with Makenna even more and demanded that she and Dante marry. Makenna never told her Da who hurt her until recently and when Granda found out, he decided to repay his wife in kind. He slit her throat and ended her miserable life.

Matteo on the other hand, died at the hands of his son. It's not public knowledge that Dante was the one to off that bastard, but he did and thankfully no one has found out and no one ever will. The world believes that the 'great' Matteo Bianchi had a heart attack. But he died knowing that his son was the one to kill him and for the Bianchi men, they're happy knowing he's dead and that his reign of raping innocent women is over.

"Do you think that Romero will want children?" I muse out loud. It's something that has been playing on my mind a lot and I'm not sure if that's something he'd want or not.

"You haven't spoken about it?" she queries, her brow raised.

I shake my head. "No, I guess I'm too scared to find out the truth. What if he never wants them?"

Makenna's lips thin into a line. "You'll never know unless you ask. Are you on birth control?"

I nod. "Yeah, I get the depo shot every eight weeks." I sigh, why am I scared to ask him? "It's not as though I want a baby right now, I just want to know about the future."

"Talk to him, Hol, it's the only way to have definitive answers."

"I'll talk to him," I promise her.

I hear Alessio's voice and I frown, shouldn't he be with Romero and Dante?

Makenna slides off the bed. "Rest, I'll be back soon. I have to rip someone a new arsehole."

I giggle, "Go easy on him, he's going through something."

We can all see that he's changed, he's cagey and distant. I had thought he had found a woman but I'm not so sure anymore.

"Rest," she repeats as she leaves my room.

I close my eyes as the tiredness starts to take over my body. I pray that Romero's okay.

THIRTEEN
ROMERO

Walking into the warehouse, I take in the scene around me. Adriano, Bosco, and Franco managed to keep their tempers in check, the asshole's hanging to the pipes above us are barely bleeding. The men spread out, each of them know that they'll not get involved. They're here to watch and they'll not be disappointed. I'm about to put on a show. One that's going to get bloody.

I roll up my sleeves, my shirt still stained with the blood of my wife. I want those assholes to know what they've done, why they're going to receive this punishment.

"Which one pulled the trigger?" My voice is deceptively calm. It's something that I have learned over the years. Keep it cool, never let them know what's about to come. Being angry and pissed isn't going to make them talk. No, these are Russian mobsters. Just as with the Italian and the Irish, our loyalty goes deep. You become Made, you take an oath. You break that oath, you're dead. There's no other way about it.

Neither man says a word, just glare at me. They're stripped down to their underwear, the muscles taught as they hang from the pipes. There's no way for them to escape, they've no weapons, and they're handcuffed, it won't be long until the muscles in their shoulders start to tear away from the weight they're under. It's going to be painful, but that'll be the least painful thing that's going to happen to them this evening.

My cell rings and as I pull it from my pocket, I'm not surprised to see Denis' name on screen. I glance at Dante and incline my head. He'll take over the questioning now.

"Yeah," I answer, my tone not welcoming, I'm pissed that he's interrupting me.

"Is she okay?" he says in lieu of greeting. "I know what my daughter is like, Romero, she downplays everything, always has."

I make note of that information, "She's with Makenna, she was grazed, it bled like a stuck pig, but she's okay."

I hear the sharp intake of breath. "Good, I'm on my way to the airport. We'll be there tomorrow."

I grind my teeth, fuck. "I can take care of my wife."

"Never said you couldn't. When you have kids, you'll know what I'm feeling. Now, Holly said that you found the bastards that shot her."

"Yep, looking at them as we speak," I murmur as I listen to Dante telling them who I'm on the phone with and what's going to happen to them.

"Good, don't take it easy on them."

I bite back the scoff. "Never do. They'll pay for what they've done as will the cunts that ordered the hit."

I hear his chuckle this time. "I always knew I liked you."

I roll my eyes. "Bullshit. Now are we done?"

"Yep," he replies, his voice filled with laughter. "I'll see you soon. Look after my baby girl."

I clench my jaw as I end the call.

"You can't end your father-in-law," Dante says quietly from beside me. "Not only will Holly hate you, Makenna will kill you for ending her brother."

I ignore him, I'm not going to kill Denis, no matter how much I would like too. Holly loves him and that's why I'll never do it.

"They're hiding something," he says changing the subject. "They know their times up."

Oh, it's up all right.

"When did the Russian's start doing business with traitors?" I question as I step forward. I see the slight unease flicker through their eyes. "The Damini's are wanted by not only the Irish, but also by us. So what would the Russian's want with those bastards?"

Wariness creeps into their features. Ah, they didn't realize that we know that those fuckers are working with the Russians. "You've got a choice," I begin, I'm lying of course, there is no fucking choice. I do whatever the hell I want to do. "You can tell us and I'll go easy on you. Give you a quick and painless death." Never going to fucking happen. "Or you can continue to act as though you don't know shit and I'll take my sweet motherfucking time and take shreds of your skin, piece by piece, I'll have you spilling your guts within hours. Then I'll make you have the most painful death you could ever imagine."

Dante nods beside me. "As he takes your skin, he'll fucking smile while doing it."

They glance at each other, I see the anger, resentment, and determination in their eyes. They're not going to go down easy.

"Excellent," I state with a fucking grin. "I was hoping you'd take the second option."

My men chuckle when I unsheathe my knife from the holster. "It's playtime," I say with a wicked smile.

I move toward the biggest and strongest of the two men, his arms and torso covered in tatts, all detailing his life with the Bratva. His muscles tense even more the closer I get toward him. "I know you bastards love the pain, I know that if I were to cut your fingers or toes off, you wouldn't give a fuck. Hell, you'd probably smile while I was doing it."

The smug smile he has tells me that I'm right.

"What about if I take your ear?" I ask with a raised brow and I enjoy watching that smugness fall from his face. "What will you do then? Hmm, I guess there's only one way to find out." I move behind him, I've got at least four inches on the bastard, so it's easy for me to reach him. He flinches when I touch his ear.

This is what I love. The fear. I thrive from it. This is what I crave. The need to see someone in pain, the urge to take their life. I have the compulsion to watch them take their last breath. Only one thing better than hearing the gasps of someone dying, it's hearing Holly as she comes. My fucking wife is my light. The only good that I have in this world. She's something to be cherished, to be adored and yet, these motherfuckers took a shot at her.

My knife hits his skin and the asshole starts to struggle. My laughter is hollow and sadistic. Nothing these bastards do will ever make me stop. The only way that'll happen is when they take their last breaths and that'll be after I have dished out the justice Holly deserves.

I slice through his skin as though it's butter, when I reach the bone and cartilage I add pressure. Our men all wear the same expression, smugness. They all have their arms crossed over their chests, their feet spread apart as they glare at the bastards hanging. It doesn't take long until I've sliced his ear off.

I move so that I'm facing them both, the prick's ear in my hand, I hold it up like a trophy and show them. Their faces pale at the sight. "This is only the beginning, I assure you; what I have planned for you both will just get worse. Now, are you ready to talk?"

Again, their stubbornness sets in and I move to the next guy. He's slimmer, less muscle and even smaller than the first guy. I look him over and decide that it's time to take their tattoos. It's the ultimate disrespect as they've earned them. Especially the stars on their knees. It means that they'll not bow to anyone, they've earned that right. These two bastards are higher up the food chain of the Russian Mafia. But still not that high, they're doing drive by shootings like they're amateurs.

"Have it your way." I throw the ear beneath their feet and get started on ridding these assholes of their stars. Skinning someone isn't easy, it's taken years of practice. The first time I did it, it was a fucking mess. Blood everywhere, the fucker died not long afterward. I didn't prolong the pain and it took me three more attempts before I learned the error of my way and realized what I was doing wrong.

Now, well now, I slice their skin away as though I'm carving meat. It comes away from the bone easily.

"*Podonok*," he spits out in Russian. I give him a blank stare. Do I look like I give a fuck what he's saying in his native tongue? "Fucker," he says in English.

I move to his other knee and start to slice that one. "You're a dead man," his accent thick and filled with pain.

"Funny," I mutter, "coming from the man that's hanging in a warehouse. I hope you kissed your wife and kids goodbye before you left today." Blood pours from his kneecaps, the skin gone and now all that remains is muscle, bones and blood.

"*Pizda*," he spits at me.

I laugh. "Told you asshole, this is only the beginning."

THREE HOURS later and these bastards still haven't given up who the fuck ordered the hit on us, or what the hell they're doing working with the Daminis. I'm glad they haven't. I'm enjoying slicing them open. It's been a while since I unleashed the beast that's hidden deep inside.

The men are panting, their body's dripping with blood, sweat, and piss. I've taken the majority of their tattoos. It pissed them off, the Russian's work hard to earn their stripes so to say, getting tattoo's means that you have proven your worth that you're somebody and I have taken everything from them. That's got to fucking sting. But they shouldn't have shot my wife.

"Now, as you have realized, I wasn't lying. I could spend the rest of the evening doing this." It's almost three in the damn morning and I want to see my wife. "But I don't think anything I do is going to make you talk. That's why I've decided to switch things up."

I click my fingers and Dante chuckles, my brother has stayed silent throughout it all. He let me lead. I know he's watching me carefully, waiting to see if I crack. That's not going to happen. I don't break. I don't fucking shatter. I'm not fragile. I'm a motherfucking monster that will do whatever the hell it takes to protect my woman.

Bosco moves forward, an electronic tablet in his hand, the screen on and our man standing by waiting for the word.

As Holly is mine, I have both Irish and Italian men with

me. They fucked with the wrong family, that's for fucking sure.

Petrov, the man that lost his ear sucks in a sharp breath as his eyes focus on the tablet screen. *"Nyet,"* he roars, his face red, his eyes wild. "No, leave them alone."

"Tell me why you're working with the Daminis?"

He glances at his friend and finally there's only despair in his eyes. "Maruzzo Damini is an asshole," his breathing is hard and coming out in pants, it's making his accent thicker and harder to understand. "He and your father worked together, worked with us. Bringing women from US to Europe."

"Trafficking?" I snarl at him and he nods. "Bastards."

Anger flashes in his eyes, "We make good money. It's a good system, easy to get them, easy to ship them. Win - win. Until your father died, now Damini thinks he can control the shipments." He turns his nose up in disgust. "Never going to happen. He came to us, told us that if we didn't help him deal with that *suka*, he'd take his business else...."

My fist is in the fucker's face before he even finishes his sentence. I'm not a fucking idiot. I know that *suka* means bitch. "Do not talk about my wife." I growl at him ready to tear his fucking head off.

He spits blood from his mouth and glares at me. "Damini's will die. No one threatens us and lives to tell the tale but your wife knows too much. She has seen the transactions between us."

Fuck. This is even worse than I thought. These bastards aren't going to stop.

"Damini told the boss that your wife will talk, that we needed to end her. Although, he did not say that she was your wife, nor the daughter of Denis Gallagher."

Why am I not surprised that the asshole is trying to save himself?

"Where can I find Maruzzo?"

He shakes his head, pain lacing his eyes. "I do not know."

I believe him.

I turn to Pitor. "What about you. Do you have anything to add?"

The man shudders, "No, both the Damini men are gunning for your wife. They'll get her eventually."

No they fucking won't.

I pull out my gun and empty two rounds into their heads.

"Clean this up and burn their bodies," Dante instructs as we move toward the exit. "I'll call Dimitri, it's time he and I had a sit down." Dimitri is the head of the Bratva, he's only just risen to succession. He's kept quiet, re-building the power the Russian's once had.

It's more than fucking time. "I'll be there." My tone brokers no arguments.

He pulls out his cell and shakes his head. "No doubt Kenna will want a play by play of what happened."

I chuckle. "That's what happens when you marry a psychopath."

"You call my wife a psycho after what I just witnessed in there?"

I scoff. "Like you wouldn't have done the same."

Dante would have gone on a damn rampage, he doesn't have finesse about it. He uses brute force and will kill anyone who dares to harm his wife, family, or organization. I on the other hand will take my time and dish out the pain, prolonging it until they're unable to take anymore.

I don't bother changing my shirt, I'll shower once I get

back to Dante and Makenna's house. I need to lay eyes on my wife, to ensure that she's okay.

Tomorrow, we'll sort the rest of this bullshit out. I'm making it my mission to take out the Daminis. They'll not get a chance to try and take out Holly again.

FOURTEEN
HOLLY

I'm woken by the door creaking open. I haven't managed to get too much sleep, constantly tossing and turning as I wait for Romero to come home. Makenna's been hovering all night, checking in on me every hour or so. I sit up ready to tell Kenna to take her pregnant arse back to bed and get some rest, but my breath is caught in my lungs as I stare at my husband.

His usual crisp white shirt, his arms, face, and his pants are covered in blood. His shirt's soaked in it. My gaze goes from his body back to his face, I don't see any pain in his eyes nor on his features, but this is Rome, he's able to mask his emotions. Even if he were in pain, I'd never know unless he tells me.

I'm moving toward him before either of us say a word. His brown eyes dark as he takes me in. His gaze follows my every step, I feel as though I'm being watched by a wild animal, one that's ready to attack at any moment. "Are you okay?" I whisper as my hand reaches out to touch him.

He withdraws. "Don't," his voice harsh.

My heart shatters, he's never rejected me before. I take a step back, unsure as to what I should do.

"I'm going to shower. Go to bed," he instructs, his eyes still dark, his voice still has that bite to it. He moves toward the bathroom and all I can do is stare at his retreating back, wondering what the hell happened.

I've caught a glimpse at the monster that everyone says lives inside of him. But I'm not scared, the man I love would never hurt me. I know that deep down in my bones. I hear the shower turn on and sigh. I have a choice to make. Do I go back to bed and act as though whatever the fuck just happened, didn't? Or do I go to him and try and make what's a shitty day, a little better?

I'm stripping out of my clothes before I even make it to the bathroom door. As I enter the bathroom, my heart stutters as I see my man standing in the shower, water cascading down his body but his heads bowed and his hands are on the tiled wall.

I silently get in behind him, reaching for the washcloth. My first touch has him freezing, his body tense, but I ignore it. I start to clean him, trying to wash away the blood and whatever else is on him.

"Doll face..." It's a warning, one that I ignore. "Holly, leave it," he says through clenched teeth.

"You are my husband," I begin, getting annoyed that he's pushing me away. "I needed you tonight, but you needed to do what you needed to do." I continue to wash him, this time when he tenses it's not because of my touch, but my words. "So, I didn't say anything, I closed my eyes and you left. Because I knew that was what you needed. You do not get to push me away, Rome. You just don't. I am your fucking wife..." My voice cracks and the tears that I have held onto all night start to slip down my face. "I am here through the good times and the bad. So, I'm going to wash you and then we're going to bed, I'm tired, I have a headache and now that you're home, I may be able to sleep."

He turns so that he's facing me, I don't move my gaze from his chest. "Doll face," he says, his voice gentle.

I shake my head. "Let me do this," I murmur as I begin to clean his chest. "Let me love you."

He rests his forehead against mine as the water washes away the shit that's happened today. We're silent, the only sounds that can be heard are the running water and our breathing.

"My turn," he says once I'm finished cleaning him and I finally raise my gaze to his face. The breath is stolen from me as I see emotion in his face. If I didn't know better, I'd have said it was love that was shining in his beautiful brown eyes.

I shake my head, slightly wincing as the pain intensifies. "I'm fine."

He pulls me into him, our body crashing against each other. "Your hair is covered in blood, lean back and I'll wash it."

I sigh and do as he asks, and I move so that I'm facing away from him so that he can wash my hair. My legs are wobbly, my entire body is tired, I'm dying to crawl back into bed and pass out. "I've got you, baby," he whispers as I lean back against him, no longer able to fully support my weight. "Did you sleep much while I was gone?"

I shake my head. "No, I was worried about you," I confess silently.

He kisses my head, but doesn't comment, he finishes washing me. I close my eyes and let him take care of me. "Let's get you dried," he whispers as he shuts the shower off and lifts me into his arms. I rest my cheek against his wet shoulder, still not opening my eyes.

"Holly, you're fucking wrecked, you should have slept."

"I couldn't when you weren't here. I've gotten used to sleeping beside you," I grumble softly and my body's jolted when he starts to silently chuckle. "Smug bastard."

"Babe..." he says his voice filled with amusement.

"Drop me on the bed, I'm too tired to get dried and dressed," I mumble as I yawn and snuggle closer into him.

"I've got you, just rest," he instructs me as he places me onto the counter and starts to dry me. He's being so bloody sweet, I can't help but open my eyes and stare at him. His hair wet and drops are falling onto his face, but he doesn't care, he's focused on taking care of me.

My gaze moves from his face to his body, he's naked and I sigh as I look at him. Wondering how it's fair that the man can be gorgeous, have an amazing body, and is so damn sweet? But then, I know that he reserves his sweetness for only me. Something that I love.

"You're supposed to be resting."

"I am," I smile softly, "I can rest while I'll ogle you."

He chuckles, it's something that I love to hear, he doesn't do it very often and I cherish it when he does.

Once he has both of us dried, he turns back to me. "What do you want to wear?" His question makes me smile wider. "You want my tee don't you?"

I roll my eyes, like he has to even ask. Some nights I love to pull on his tee and sleep. Others, I put on my silky nightgown, which Rome always seems to strip from me.

"Okay, doll face." He leaves me on the counter and moves to the bedroom. When he comes back minutes later, he's in his underwear and has a tee in his hands.

Once he has me dressed, I cling to him, my legs and

arms around him. "Come on, let's go to bed." His hands go to my arse as he walks us into the bedroom.

As soon as we're in bed, he pulls me into him. His arms tight around my body. I settle against him, feeling relieved, safe, and secure. That's something that I've felt around Rome since we've been married. I'm a lucky girl. I've been surrounded my entire life by men who'll do whatever they can to protect me.

"They're dead, doll face," he says softly after a few moments of silence. "I'm going to fix this."

I nestle into him further, understanding the words he didn't say. This isn't over, there's still people out there that want to hurt me.

"Why did you try to push me away?" I ask into his neck.

"You're so fucking pure. So fragile. I don't want any of my shit tainting you. It's bad enough that you have to deal with this life, nothing should touch you. When you came toward me and tried to touch me, all I could think about was their blood tainting you."

Oh, God.

"Love you," I whisper thickly, trying to keep the tears at bay. "So much."

His arms tighten around me, I raise my head and stare at him, loving the adoration he has in his eyes for me. The air starts to crackle around us, I need him.

"Doll face..." the worry is clear to hear in his voice.

I shake my head, "I'm fine, I'm alive. I need to feel that, Rome, I need you."

His lips crash down against mine; my pulse quickens as my fingers tangle into his hair. God, I want this man so much, I've never felt the need that I have whenever Romero touches me.

His tongue sweeps into my mouth taking my breath

away. He pulls me closer, my fingers tightening against his hair. Our bodies flush against each other, my skin feels as though it's burning, I crave his touch so much.

He rolls me onto my back, quickly removing the tee from my body before sliding between my legs. His cock thick against my stomach, I grind against him, needing to feel the friction. Needing that touch, that only he can give me. Our tongues caressing one another, as the kiss deepens. I moan deep in my throat as his finger skims my thigh, my stomach does a flip while heat pools between my legs.

"Please, hon," I plead with him.

His eyes darkened with lust and I know that he's not going to deny me. He thrusts against my pussy, his mouth once again on mine. The sensory overload is too much, I'm clawing at his back while I grind against him trying to take what I'm so desperately craving but my husband knows my needs better than I do. He's out of his boxers in a blink of an eye, positioning himself at my entrance.

"Doll face, so wet, so fucking good, so mine." He slams into me, he's too big, too thick. God, so good. I'm meeting him thrust for thrust. His calloused hands groping my body, touching every inch of skin, leaving me burning for him.

"Rome," I gasp, when he takes one of my nipples into his mouth, swirling his tongue around the erected nipple, nipping, sucking, tasting. He's driving me wild, I'm mewling, panting, begging for more as I feel my orgasm start to build. His cock pounding into me relentlessly, as he too tries to find his release.

"Never had anyone love me," he begins, and my heart hurts at hearing those words. He thrusts into me again, harder, more powerful than before, as though he's trying to get as far inside of me as he possibly can. "Never had anyone care for me before," he needs to stop, his words are too much. "Never felt what you've given me. A home. A life. Love."

His hands grip my arse cheeks, and he pounds into me. My orgasm climbing, I'm reaching heights that I've never gone to before. "You've made my world fill with color. Before you, it was death and blood."

I detonate. His name a cry on my lips as I break apart.

He continues to thrust into me, his body tight and his grip punishing, but it's Rome, it's his way of showing me his affection, via fucking. I can't deny that it's what I want, what I need, what I love.

"Beauty," he says, his words tight, "that's what I get now. What I wake up to every fucking morning. Fuck," he growls as his cock expands inside of me and he releases hot spurts of cum in my pussy.

We collapse into an exhausted heap, both of us panting, unable to release the other. His cock still rooted in me. "Love you, Rome," I whisper as my eyes flutter close. "I'm so sorry that you weren't appreciated before, but I vow, hon, that every day for the rest of my life, I'll show you just how much you mean to me. How much I love you."

His voice is gruff when he responds, it takes everything I have not to burst into tears at his words. "I hate that I'm hurting you. I have no idea of what love is."

"You're not hurting me," I promise him. "I know that you care about me, and Rome, I love that. You protect me, you make me feel safe, and you'd never hurt me. That's all that I could ever ask of you." Do I want him to love me? Yes, but I'll live with what he can give me.

He kisses my hair, and I sink further into his embrace. "Can I ask you something?" I murmur into his chest.

"As long as it's not about my parents, then yes," his tone

isn't angry or unpleasant, it's normal. It makes me desperate to find out what his parents did to him.

"I won't push you to talk about them and what happened, but I hope you tell me someday."

He squeezes me letting me know that he heard, "You had a question?"

"Do you want kids?"

His body tenses, his arms around me getting heavier. "Are you pregnant?"

I roll my eyes, Jesus, how the hell did he get that from my question? "No, Rome, I'm not. I'm on birth control. I'm not ready for kids, not yet, probably not for a few years."

He releases a breath and I'd laugh if my stomach wasn't so tense. "I don't want them yet. Someday, sure, but not yet."

I kiss his chest, happy that he wants them. I'd have been okay if he hadn't, it would have been a blow, but not something I couldn't deal with.

"Sleep now, doll face. Your dad will be here in the morning." He kisses my head once more.

I smile, knowing that tomorrow, I'm going to have three men I love the most in this world under one roof. God, I've missed Da and Danny.

"Night, Rome, love you," I say on a yawn as my eyes droop.

FIFTEEN
ROMERO

I'm pissed. Beyond fucking pissed. I woke up ten minutes ago to find Holly no longer in bed with me, nor was she in the bathroom. Glancing at my watch, I see that it's almost noon. Fuck. No wonder she was gone from our bed. The smell of bacon and eggs hits me as soon as I open the bedroom door.

Making my way downstairs, the voices with thick Irish accents tell me that Holly's family are here. "Ah, Romero, you're awake, good," Denis says when he sees me.

HOLLY'S at the stove cooking, a bright smile on her face. She looks relaxed, what happened yesterday pushed aside and now she's dressed in my tee, and only my tee.

I STALK TOWARD HER, she follows my every step, not once taking her gaze from me. The smile she had frozen in place as she tilts her head to study me, no doubt trying to gauge my mood. Pissed. That's what I am. First, she was gone when I woke up, that doesn't fucking happen and now she's standing in a room full of men wearing nothing but my tee.

"WHAT THE FUCK ARE YOU WEARING?" I ask her as I walk into her space. My words are snarled at her.

SHE FROWNS AT ME. She has a confused look on her face. "What's wrong, hon?"

IS SHE FOR FUCKING REAL? "WRONG?" I ask, my voice vibrating with anger. "Where's your clothes?"

HER FROWN MORPHS INTO A SCOWL. "I'm wearing clothes, Romero!" She crosses her arms over her chest and glares at me. The fact that she called me Romero, tells me how pissed she is right now. "Whatever the fuck your problem is, take it elsewhere. I'm busy."

I RAISE A BROW, reminding her to remember who the fuck she's talking too. "You're in my tee," I say clearly, "only my fucking tee."

HER EYES FLASH WITH ANGER, it's a sight to behold. Very rarely does she get angry and when she does, it's beautiful.

. . .

"I'M WEARING UNDERWEAR," she hisses at me. "This is my family. Our family. No one cares what the fuck I'm wearing. I shouldn't feel ashamed of wearing clothes. Besides what the hell am I supposed to wear a bin bag?"

"THAT fucker not too long ago made it clear he wanted you, I do not want a repeat of it."

SHE SMIRKS AT MY WORDS. "Yeah, well, I've had to deal with that whore making a play for you at every opportunity, but I don't say shit to you about what to wear." She shakes her head in disgust. "You can finish breakfast, I have to change." She turns and walks away, leaving me standing at the stove wondering how the fuck she turned it around on me.

LAUGHTER HAS me turning and pinning a glare at my brother. "Where the fuck were you last night?" I ask Alessio, he never turned up at the warehouse.

I SEE Dante and Makenna share a glance, obviously they're communicating silently. "What the fuck happened?" I demand.

"I'LL SORT THE BREAKFAST OUT," Denis says as he comes to stand beside me, "you sort out, whatever the fuck that is. My daughter loves you, Romero, she really does, don't be an arsehole to her, she doesn't deserve it. She was worried about you, Dante wanted to wake you as he wanted to organize the meet with Dimitri, but Holly wasn't having any of it, she pitched a fit and made sure no one went near you, that you needed sleep."

FUCK.

"YOU'RE GOING to be pissed when you find out what Alessio has to say and when Holly finds out she's going to be hurt."

I NARROW MY EYES, what the fuck happened?

I GIVE him a chin lift before moving toward my brothers. "Want to tell me what I'm missing."

MAKENNA SIGHS. "This is where I'll leave you be. I'm going to check in on Danny and Lissa." She turns to walk away. "One of you are going to tell Holly, I'm not telling her. She's dealt with that bitch enough."

I NARROW my eyes on my brothers. "Someone had better start talking."

"I FUCKED UP," Ales says, and I clench my jaw, how many times am I going to hear that?

. . .

"LAST NIGHT, HE SLEPT WITH GEORGINA," Dante informs me, and I pin my idiot younger brother with a gaze filled with hatred. "Not only that, he overheard her say that she's going to get even with Holly for taking away her man."

I CLENCH MY JAW. What the fuck is wrong with that motherfucking bitch? I never once treated her like anything but a quick and easy fuck. There was no finesse about it. A quick fumble whenever I needed to get my rocks off, or needed her mouth wrapped around my cock.

"I THINK that she's planning something," Alessio tells me and I'm so fucking close to snapping his neck. "I know that she's a bitch, but I don't see why you're all fucking angry about it. I mean, you don't even like her."

I TURN TO DANTE, needing him to sort this out before I do something like pull my knife and slit the fucker's throat.

"IT'S NOT Rome that we're worried about. It's Holly. Don't you think she's got enough to worry about dealing with the fucking Damini's trying to end her along with the Russians. Which is, your fucking fault for opening your damn mouth, but she also has to deal with a fucking bitch that doesn't realize her place in this world."

. . .

HE OPENS his mouth as if he's going to justify what he's done but I cut him off. "If that cunt comes near my wife, I don't give a fuck, I'm ending her. She's been warned time and time again."

"HOLLY WILL BE HURT that you fucked her, but that's because the woman's actively trying to get back into Romero's bed," Denis says inserting himself into our conversation. "It takes a lot before Holly will blow, and gentleman, she's close to that point." He has a fucking huge grin on his face, as though he's looking forward to her losing her temper.

THE DOORBELL RINGS and I frown, where's the damn guards?

"I'LL GET IT," Holly calls out, I hear her footsteps on the stairs.

"DON'T," I yell, something in my gut is saying that this isn't right. But it's too late, she's already at the door. I glance at Denis and see the narrowing of his eyes as he takes the skillet off the stove. Both he and I are on the move before my brothers can say a word.

"WHAT THE FUCK are you doing here?" Holly growls. Actually fucking growls.

. . .

I ROUND the corner in time to see Georgina step into the house sporting a smile. She glances at me at the smile turns sinister. "Oh, Romero, there you are."

THE BITCH OPENS her jacket to show that she's wearing nothing but her lingerie. Fucking cunt. She grins as she takes the jacket off and throws it to the floor.

"JESUS," Danny's gruff voice snarls as he steps into the room. "Desperate much?"

"SOMEONE HAD BETTER SORT THAT FUCKING bitch out before I do," Makenna threatens.

"TIME FOR YOU TO LEAVE," Holly announces as she grips hold of Georgina's arm and drags her outside, leaving the bitch's jacket lying on the ground.

MAKENNA, Danny, and Denis are all smirking. "Lis," Danny calls out and within seconds his wife walks out of Makenna's office with their daughter Annalise in her arms, "you'd be pissed if you missed this."

SHE RAISES her brow and then looks past us to where Holly's standing, blocking Georgina from coming back into the house. "Is that the whore that doesn't understand that Romero's married?"

. . .

"YEP, she'd also be the woman that Alessio fucked last night," Makenna sneers as she glares at my brother.

HOLLY TURNS HER HEAD, her eyes flashing with hurt as she too glares at Alessio. Fuck.

GEORGINA SMIRKS. "Aww, poor Holly is jealous."

HOLLY SCOFFS. "Not in the slightest. Disappointed, yes. Wondering if I should bring Alessio to get tested, definitely. What I don't get, Georgie," Holly taunts and I smirk, "is what you thought you'd accomplish by sleeping with Alessio. I mean, we all know that you love Romero, and that you're desperate to do anything to get back into his bed. Which he's made clear would never happen, did you think you'd make him jealous by sleeping with his brother?"

GEORGINA'S SMIRK falls from her face.

"YOU CAN'T BE THAT STUPID," Melissa comments. "No guy wants a woman that's been with his brother."

"IF ROMERO WANTED YOU, he'd have had you by now, he hasn't, he doesn't want you. It's time for you to move the fuck on," Makenna snaps as she takes a step forward.

"BITCH," Georgina snarls, "don't talk to me like that, little Miss sunshine here isn't all that and Romero will be back to me." She steps forward so that she's inches away from Holly, "How does it feel knowing that you're second best?"

"OH, DARLING," Holly smiles at her, "I'm no one's second best. He married me, whereas he used you. You're always going to be the bridesmaid, never the bride." And with that parting shot, Holly cocks her arm back and pushes her fist forward, smashing it into Georgina's face. "Now, you've been asked to leave. Nicely, I may add. Do it, before the niceties end."

TO MAKE IT EVEN WORSE, Holly slams the door in her face. "Breakfast?" She asks with a smirk.

I PULL her into my arms. "That's some right hook you've got, doll face."

SHE BEAMS AT ME, "It is and don't you forget it."

"HOW THE HELL did I not know that Holly packed a mean punch?" Alessio asks.

. . .

"HOW DID I not know that you were that desperate?" she returns, and I chuckle.

"I FOR ONE am glad that she's okay," Melissa says as she pulls Holly from me and into an embrace. "I thought Danny was going to kill people. When Denis called last night, Danny lost his mind."

"SO DID DA," Danny grunts.

"DO you know what it's like to find out your daughter's been shot and you're across the fucking Atlantic?"

"I'M FINE, I'm just pleased you left Ma at home."

"I THINK you've had enough of one bitch for the day," Denis replies. "Besides, your Ma has no idea I'm here."

I TAKE a seat and pull Holly onto my lap, she settles against me and sighs, "Da, how the hell did you manage to sneak out the house without Ma knowing?" Holly asks, her head resting against my shoulder.

"I WASN'T at home when you called."

. . .

DANNY, Melissa, Makenna, and Holly all have matching grins. "You have a woman?" Holly says excitedly.

"PLEASE, fuck, please tell me you do," Danny pleads.

"OF COURSE, HE HAS," Melissa says, "that's why he's been spending all his time with us. It's not because of Annalise, it's because he's got a woman. What she like?"

DENIS GLARES AT THEM, not bothering to answer them.

"BUT DA," Holly whines and I shake my head, she's so fucking spoilt when it comes to her family. "Is she nice?"

"FUCK," he grunts. "Yes, she's nice. I've been seeing her for about four months and no, you can't meet her."

DANNY NARROWS HIS EYES, "WHY?"

"BECAUSE SHE'S YOUR AGE."

HOLLY'S MOUTH FALLS OPEN. "But Da, do you like her?" Denis grunts, "Do you love her?" This time he doesn't acknowledge that he heard her. "If you like her, who cares how old she is?"

HIS EYES SOFTEN at his daughter's words. "We'll see."

HOLLY TENSES AGAINST ME. "Da, she does know about Ma, right?"

"BREAKFAST," he says and just like that, everyone's mood plummets. It's fucking weird that they're all happy that he's found a woman even though he's married to a fucking bitch. I don't blame him for looking elsewhere, Zoe has done it for the past two decades. But not letting the woman know is a fucking shit thing to do and this can only go one way. It's going to shatter around him.

SIXTEEN
ROMERO

"You sure about this?" I ask Dante as Stefan drives us toward the meet with Dimitri.

He spears me with a piercing look, my brother hates being questioned, but right now, he needs to be. "Don't ask me that shit again. I don't need you on my back too. This is family business and as you damn well know, I'm head of this family."

That tone has no effect on me. I'm well aware of what my brother can achieve, just how ruthless he can be. I'm not pissed that he talks about himself that way, it's the way he should be talking about himself. He is the motherfucking boss. Anyone who doesn't treat him that way is considered disrespectful and, in our world, being disrespectful means you lose your tongue.

"I'm not questioning you." Bullshit, I totally am, I think the man lost his damn mind somewhere between that fucking bitch showing up at his front door looking for me and having breakfast. "I'm just saying that this is our brother, Dante."

He shakes his head, "Listen to me, Rome. You're both

my brother's and I'd do whatever the fuck I had to in order to protect you. But when you put people in danger, especially someone as close to this family as Holly is, then I cannot protect him. I thought of all people you'd be fully on board with this."

"Oh, I want to kneecap the bastard so bad, but Holly would be pissed, and Makenna would go for my balls if I got blood on your floor. But a test? Surely he's not that stupid to fail it."

As soon as the words leave my mouth, I know that he is that fucking stupid.

"While the Gallagher's are here, I've asked them to do some recon work for me."

Damn it.

"They're tailing him?" I can't keep the bite out of my tone. That's a fucking shitty thing to do.

Dante sighs, he's getting annoyed with my constant questioning. "Rome, seriously?" He sneers at me; I can't help but stifle a smile. "Fucking ass," he mutters having seen the amusement on my face. "Yes, they're tailing him."

He reaches into his pocket and pulls out an envelope and throws it to me. "Look, and then try and disagree that this is the best decision."

Opening the envelope, pictures spill out, one in particular catches my eye instantly. My gut tightens as I realize the implications if this image ever becomes public.

"What the fuck?"

"Keep looking," he instructs and I'm wondering what else could be worse than what I've just seen.

But then, I realize that there's a whole fucking lot that is worse. When I put the pictures back into the envelope, I hand it back to Dante and hit the button to bring the partition down. This is a conversation between Dante and I, as much as Stefan has proven himself, I don't trust him with the knowledge of what those pictures hold.

"He's in bed with the fucking Russians?" I can't keep the utter contempt from my voice. I'm fucking pissed. My brother in bed with the fucking Russians. God, there's nothing fucking worse. Oh, wait... "What the fuck is he doing with drugs?"

Dante sighs. "Now do you understand why I set up the test?"

I would have forgone the test and put a bullet in the fucking bastard. God, our fucking brother. Did he really not have an idea what he was doing when he spoke about Holly's work? Or was it a ploy to sneak under the radar and fuck us over?

"Who the fuck is the woman?" I ask, wondering who my brother's sleeping with. The woman has the Russian insignia tattooed on her ribs.

Dante shakes his head. "I have no fucking idea, Makenna and Melissa are working on it as we speak. I'm keeping this close to the fucking chest. No one outside of the immediate family are to know about this."

I lean my head back against the seat. "When the fuck did the Irish become immediate family?" Holly is my family. Not her fucking father and brother.

Dante grins. "You always hated sharing. Anyway, they wanted to help and having them look into it, means that if it's as bad as the pictures seem, then we can deal with it first before it becomes public knowledge."

"Yeah, and what if he's in bed with the Russians? What then?" I demand to know. If he is, I'm going to kill him. I won't even hesitate to slit his fucking throat. If he is working with them, that means he's against us and that's something neither Dante or I can allow to continue, nor can we let him live. If he has been betraying us, he's the reason that Holly has been shot and why she's got those Dimani assholes after her, for that alone, I'll slit his throat.

I never thought that I'd put anyone or anything above the *family,* but that was until Holly. I'd fucking kill, maim, destroy anyone that stands to harm her. That includes my brothers. I'm okay with that, Holly, she's so fucking pure, she's worth it. I'd do whatever the fuck I had to ensure her safety and I'd have no regrets in doing so.

"If he's betrayed us," Dante begins, his voice vibrating with anger and menace. "There's no place on earth he'd be able to hide." He turns to me, this time he's looking at me as a brother. Not the boss. "Whatever the fuck's wrong with him has to do with Dad. He started changing after that day."

I nod in agreement, I noticed that too. "It's not as though he hasn't killed anyone before. Hell, he's killed more than his fair share." Alessio, just as the rest of us, had been brought up to embrace death, to view it more as a friend than a foe.

I've fully embraced it, when my time comes, it comes but I'll go down fucking swinging, taking out as many assholes as I can. I won't go down like my dad did, killed by family. Fuck no. I learned that at a young age. Family is everything. Dante and Alessio are my family. This life and the men are my family.

Stefan pulls up out front of the restaurant owned by none other than fucking Carter. But as a Syndicate the fucker is trying to get into everyone's good graces and is sucking up hard. He has a restaurant that's in the middle of our territory and so far, he's managed to be as neutral as can be, he's not looked for an alliance with either us or the Russians that we know of.

Dante isn't stupid and as soon as this meet was set up, our men set up around the restaurant ready in case anything pops off and the way I'm feeling today, I'll be putting a bullet in Carter's fucking head and then Dimitri's.

"Show time." Dante flashes me his shark's grin. "These fuckers are going to end the hit on Holly, or I'll end them."

I smirk. "Here's hoping they don't agree with you." It's been a while since I've let loose. Same for Dante. Since he married Makenna, he's had to take a step back while Makenna finds her feet and our men recognize her as their boss. He doesn't mind that he's had to do that, he and Makenna are building a fucking empire, something that no one else can rival and they're succeeding. The Irish are taking over the Midwest quicker than anticipated and knowing them and the way they work, they'll soon take over the West in no time.

Three black escalades are parked at the end of the block. Anyone looking at them will think they belong to Carter, the fucker loves his escalades, every single one of his men drive them. But sitting in those Escalades are fifteen of our men, ready to jump out when they receive word. Altogether, we have about seventy men positioned in and around the restaurant.

Walking into the restaurant I see that it's been cleared out, the only people that are here are Carter's men and Dimitri's men. Twenty altogether. Hell, Dante, Stefan, and I could take them alone. Carter's gaze sweeps the men that are with us. Seven altogether along with Dante and I. We'd be fools not to bring any extra back up with us.

"Ah, Mr Bianchi," Carter says in greeting to Dante. "Can I get you something to drink?"

Dante doesn't acknowledge him and I want to smile. It's the ultimate insult. Being on someone's property and not greeting them. Mix in the fact that Carter is head of the Carter Syndicate it further adds fuel to the fire. His men all tense, but don't say anything, obviously have been warned not to start shit. Knowing Carter, he's probably hoping that we'll go to war that way he can muscle in on our territory. Fucking ass.

Dante sits down across from Dimitri, our men spread out across the restaurant, every single one of them on edge. Dimitri smirks and I grit my teeth. This is Dante's show. No matter how much this man pisses me off, I'm under Dante's rule and I'll do as he says.

"What can I do for you, Dante?" Dimitri asks, his words heavily accented.

"Well, that depends, Dimitri. Do you think working with the Dimani's would give you the edge to overthrow me?"

Dimitri's smirk falls. "Those fuckers. I do not do business with them. Your father. Yes. Those assholes. No."

I sit back and watch him carefully. My father seemed to have his hands in a lot of things. None of them are good. We don't sell women. Hell, we don't hurt them either.

"Want to explain to me why you have put a hit out on my sister-in-law?" The calmness in Dante's voice is just for show, my brother would put a bullet in Dimitri's head without breaking a sweat all while sitting in his seat. One wrong word from the bastard Russian and this is all over.

"Apologies on your nuptials," the fucker says to me and I want to fly over the table and snap his fucking neck. "Must be bad times if you're marrying the Irish *Shlyukhi*. Not one but two brothers." he shakes his head in disgust.

Dante moves before anyone can blink and pulls the trigger. The bullet sinks between Dimitri's eyes. "Now, the next person to disrespect my wife will get the same treatment," he announces, his gun still in his hands. "Who's the boss?"

The Russians glance around at each other, their eyes wide as though they can't understand why Dante's asking. A heavily scarred man steps forward. His hair is as black as his eyes. The man's fucking dead inside. This makes more sense, not the asshole that's currently slumped in front of us.

"Name?" Dante barks and the fucker smiles. "What. Is. Your. Name?"

The smile widens, does this fucker not realize how close he is to dying? "Maksim," the fucker responds. "I'm surprised, Dante, it didn't take you long to understand."

My brother scoffs. "Understand the disrespect..."

Maksim's eyes narrow. "I have respect, but those who I do not know, they have to earn it. I do not know you. But you are smart."

I want to roll my eyes. Fucking A. This is all bullshit. They're playing a very dangerous game right now.

"Explain the fucking cloak and daggers bullshit. I came for a sit down with the Pakhan." Dante's teeth are clenched, I'm surprised he hasn't chipped any. "Instead, I'm given a fucking asshole who doesn't know when to keep his mouth shut."

"Dimitri was my Brigadier," Maksim tells us. "He was a liability."

When Maksim talks, his men stand up taller, I realize now that Dimitri never had their respect. No wonder Maksim sent him into the lion's den, especially if they believed he was a liability.

"Why have someone lead your men if they're a liability..." The accusation in Dante's tone is telling, he's pissed. Beyond fucking pissed. The Bratva showed disrespect to him and that's not something that any of us are willing to let slide. One man is dead and if Maksim doesn't start talking soon, he will be too.

That'll mean a full on war between the Italians and the Russians.

Like I give a fuck.

They went after my wife. Put a fucking price on her head. They do not get a pass.

"Our lives have an expiry date..." Maksim says, every one of his men are filled with rapt attention. Eagerly awaiting this story, seems as though we weren't the only ones left in the dark. "When the time comes, Mr. Bianchi, who will take over your empire? The one that has somehow managed to grow in the past four months since your father's untimely demise. Who would you trust to continue the legacy that you have created?" His accent thick and heavy as he poses the question.

"My brother would."

Pride fills me. I've never wanted to be Capo. That's always been Dante's. He's the one that our father molded, he was the one that was treated as though he was the heir to the underworld and I was okay with that, I've done whatever I could to ensure that his place is secure. I'll always protect him and our family.

Maksim nods. "I thought the same about Dimitri..." Fuck. "But, he was too greedy. He wanted things that did not belong to him. He was not the man I thought."

"So you set him up, knowing that he was a disrespectful fuck..." I say with a raised brow and Maksim only smirks. "That was ballsy, we could have taken you all out."

He tilts his head to the side as he studies me. "That is true, but, you do not want war with me. You want your wife safe. That is something that I can understand. Women.

They do not touch our world." He glares at Dante who returns the smirk. "I assure you, that no one will harm your wife."

I glare at him. Does he expect me to believe that he'll not exact revenge for what happened here today? That they'll stop their hunt for Holly?

"You have no reason to believe me, but maybe, this may help?" He reaches into his pocket, my hand ready to go for my knife if he thinks he can take any of us out. I'm faster than him, I'd have his throat slit before he could even point the gun at us.

He pulls out his cell phone and taps the screen.

A tattooed man stands with a gun in his hand. The man leaves the screen and that's when I see them, Maruzzo and Maxim Damini.

"No, please," Maruzzo pleads, he's on his knees, his hands bound behind him. His son weeping beside him.

"Too late." The tattooed man says and fires the gun. The bullets sink between the eyes of each of the Daminis, their mouths open wide with shock as the life leaves their eyes.

Maksim puts his cell away. "Call it a peace offering. Had I known that she was your wife, I would have put an end to this. Please pass on my apology to Holly."

My teeth grind at him using my wife's name.

"Peace offering?" Dante questions. He too seems to be having a hard time believing that there'll be no come back for Dimitri's death.

Maksim rises and his men follow. "Yes, a peace offering. But Dante, piss me off, and we'll go to war."

Dante glares at him. "Oh, Maksim, you do not want to threaten me."

The fucker merely smiles. "Until next time. Please, send my regards to your wives."

"I'll fucking kill him," I grind out, pissed as fuck that the asshole thinks it's okay to talk about my wife as though he knows her.

"Not before I do. Fucking slick fuck," Dante says as we rise, I'm ready to get the fuck out of here and home to Holly.

The Russian's have already left. Carter's hovering as though he wants to say something but neither Dante nor I are in the mood to listen to him ramble about shit. I'm still pissed at what happened this morning, watching Holly punch the fucking bitch sure as fuck made it a whole lot better.

Who knew my wife had such a good right hook?

As we walk back to our vehicle, the unsettled feeling that I had is back with vengeance. A war is coming and I sure as fuck hope that whoever's planning on trying to take us down knows what they're up against. None of us will go down without a fight. I'll tear anyone a part who dares to even try.

SEVENTEEN
HOLLY

It's been two days since that skank turned up at Makenna's house dressed in her underwear and we've not heard from her since. Rome's confident that I put her in her place when I punched her, I however don't believe she's run away with her tail between her legs. I have a sickening feeling she'll be back and when she does, she'll turn her bitchiness up another notch.

"So..." Makenna drawls, her gaze moving across the room. We've all been summoned. Every Irish family member that's in the US and that's a whole lot of us, seeing as Da, Danny, and Melissa are still here.

"We've not heard anything from the Russian's and while I'd like to believe they're all for a peace offering, I'm not that trusting and I call bullshit."

Jade's gaze collides with mine and she rolls her eyes. She's annoyed she's had to fly in from Chicago with the rest of her family. Her court case is in a few months and if she's caught out of town, she'll be in even more trouble than she is. But Makenna and Dante insisted that every Irish and Italian family member be in attendance.

"We still need to be cautious. That's why the females aren't to be alone anymore..." Jade's eyes flash with anger, Makenna holds up her hand before she can protest. "I know, I hate it just as much as you do, but Jade, this is only temporary."

Jade nods stiffly, agreeing to the terms.

"Good, so as I was saying, no woman will be alone. So, Holly, Jade, and Edwina will have guards whenever they leave the house. No exception. Today, Holly and Jade are going shopping, Finn and Da will be escorting them as will Malachy, Reilly, and Boz."

Five guards? What the hell?

Romero's hand rests on my nape and I turn to him, his gaze firmly on my auntie, but I know he can sense me looking at him. I narrow my eyes at him and the cocky fucker smiles.

Makenna continues to talk about the new measures the family will be going through and what will happen if we go out without guards. She was saying that more so to Jade than the rest of us.

"Finn, Da," she says as she looks at her brother and father, "stick close to them today."

I guess I'm not the only one that has this sickening feeling in my gut that something bad is coming. Everyone has been on edge, especially Rome, which makes me feel even more anxious.

"Doll face," Romero says softly as the others get ready to leave. "Please stay close to Finn and Seamus."

I resist the urge to roll my eyes, how many times am I going to have the same thing repeated to me. "Rome, even if I were stupid, which I'm not. Do you think Granda or Uncle Finn would let me out of their sights? No. So please, relax, I'll be gone two hours tops and then I'll be back."

I hear laughter and turn to glare at Da, his shoulders shaking with laughter. Both Danny and Melissa have amused smiles on their faces. They know what I'm like when I shop. "Baby-girl, you have a shopping addiction. Since you were old enough to walk you'd shop like you were born to do it. I doubt you've ever gone shopping and managed to be back within two hours," Da says through his laughter.

I narrow my eyes at him. "Shut up."

He winks at me. "I've got to go, I'll see you later. Be safe."

My heart's heavy. Everyone is so on edge.

"You too," I say, my voice not as strong as I'd hoped. Da hesitates for a moment before he places a kiss against my forehead and then he's gone.

I turn back to Romero. "I'll be fine, I'll call you once I'm back."

He sighs heavily. "I know, I wish you could stay here," he places a kiss against my cheek, it's soft and filled with tenderness.

"I'll be quick, I need to get some things for Makenna and some new underwear, but then I'll be back," I promise him, knowing I'll do everything in my power to be back as quickly as possible, once I am back, he'll fret less.

"Thanks, doll face." His lips descend on mine and my fingers clutch his suit jacket, pulling him closer to me. I need the kiss deepened, I want to feel that breathless feeling I get when Rome gets carried away, I want that soul searing kiss, the one that I feel all the way to my bones, the one that makes my toes curl.

Romero doesn't disappoint, as soon as our tongues touch, he deepens it. We're lost in each other, our tongues caressing one another that is until there's a harsh coughing sound which breaks us apart.

"May want to let her breathe," Finn says, amusement etched in his words.

I turn to look at my uncle, the only one who has welcomed me and my family with open arms. Patrick and Cian, still to this day are closed off and wary around us. I don't care. We did nothing wrong. Granda Seamus fell in love with our granny and Da was born, but Granda Henry had other ideas and had him marry Makenna's mam who was even worse than my own Ma, which is some feat. So Da was born and we never saw Granda Seamus until Makenna married Dante. Now we're one big, dysfunctional family.

"Jealous, Finny?" Jade says with a smirk. She, like Makenna and I, gets along with Finn. Although she has a better relationship with him than I do, that's just the way Jade is, she gets along with everyone.

He grins at her and once again, I'm curious as to how he's still single. Finn is handsome, he's got the same red hair as I do, he's chiseled, fit, and his smile brightens the entire room. He's the eldest of the Gallagher brothers, he's thirty-three.

"You girls ready?" he asks not answering Jade's question if he's jealous or not.

Jade and I exchange glances and smile. "Yes, we're ready, is Granda?" I ask, having not seen him since the rest of the family left.

"He's sorting out the guards. He's taking this seriously, as should the two of ye."

I cross my arms over my chest as I narrow my eyes at him. "You think we don't feel the same thing that everyone else is feeling? We know you're all gearing up for a war, and we're not stupid, so I'd appreciate it if you'd stop treating us as though we are."

His lips curl up at the ends as though he's trying to hide his smile. "Come on, the sooner we leave, the sooner we'll be back and that'll mean I won't have your husband breathing down my neck." He shakes his head but continues to fight his smile. It's one of the things that I love about Finn, he can be so easy going and fun to be around. He never makes me feel as though I'm unwelcome.

"Hol, I'll see you in the car, I've got to speak to Da before we leave," Jade says but I have a feeling that's more so Rome and I can have some alone time before we leave.

"Doll face," Romero says softly and I turn to face him, his gaze burning into my skin, "you'll be safe." It's a promise, a vow. "Nothing is going to hurt you." He pulls me into his chest and wraps his arms around me. "I'm not sure how long I'll be gone..."

I shake my head, "It's fine, Jade and I will catch up. It's been a while." I sink further into his embrace. "Be safe, Rome. I love you. I'll be pissed if you came home hurt or worse."

His body shakes with his chuckles, the sound of his laughter is a balm to my soul.

"While you're shopping, get some of those sexy nighties, yeah?" He places a chaste kiss against my lips and I wish we could say fuck it and go back to bed.

"Be safe," I repeat again, that nagging feeling in full force.

"Always, doll face. I'll see you soon."

I blink back the tears, somehow emotional with our goodbye. "Count on it. Love you."

His eyes blaze with so much emotion it hurts my chest. "Be good." Then he's gone and the feeling inside intensifies.

God, what's going to happen? I've never been so frightened before. I can only pray that everyone I love comes home in one piece and is alive.

"HAVE TO SAY," Granda begins with a smile, "I expected it to be a hell of a lot worse than that."

I roll my eyes, I am not that fucking bad. "Don't worry, Granda, once all this shit is over with, I'll let loose, you'll have a great time."

We're sitting in the car in Makenna and Dante's driveway waiting for Finn, Malachy, Reilly, and Boz to do their walk through, making sure everything is okay.

Granda's nose crinkles, "Not that I don't love you and all, but I'd rather face a hail of bullets than go shopping."

"That can be arranged," Jade quips, her lips twitching.

He shakes his head. "You're worse than your brother. That boy has no respect."

Jade grins wide. "Uncle Seamus, you love us really. You used to tell Hayden how much you wished he was your son, because the younger two were gobshites."

Well ain't that the bloody truth. Finn is Seamus' second eldest and he's the nicest of the brother's. My Da's the oldest and then there's Patrick and Cian, both of whom are arseholes.

Granda's eyes narrow on her. "Girl, what did we agree on?"

She bites her lips, her eyes dancing with laughter. "We do not repeat each other's secrets."

"Exactly. Now, you wouldn't want your father to know about you and Jacob."

She gasps. God, I love this family, even when there's something looming over us, we're as close as ever.

"Uncle Seams," she shouts in outrage. "You bastard!"

Granda chuckles. "Now you're lucky Finn didn't hear, he'd be demanding to know what happened."

She glares at him. "Arsehole."

The passenger's side door opens and there's Finn, Malachy, Reilly, and Boz waiting for us.

"Holly and Jade behind me, Boz and Reilly either side of them, with Da and Malachy following up the rear," Finn barks, he's all focused, making sure nothing will happen to us.

Malachy helps me out of the car, while Boz and Reilly have their backs to the door, their gazes sweeping the area, watching, waiting, ready to attack and protect if need be.

As soon as my feet touch the ground, the feeling I've had all day, the one that has been humming through the air like electricity for days, intensifies, I'm not the only one to feel it. The men's backs straighten, all of them have their guns out, fingers ready to pull the trigger.

Something's coming.

I clutch Jade's hand tightly as she comes to stand beside me. Her nails biting into my skin with the grip she has on me.

"No one backs off," Finn says, "you stay tight to the girls, anything happens, Hol, Jade, you're to run into the house and into the safe room. If we don't make it, you do that, do you understand."

My heart is pounding, blood rushes through my veins at what he's saying. But I nod.

"Let's go." He takes the lead, his gun trained ahead of him.

The air is static, my fear palpable. I'm so fucking scared and yet I have no idea what it is that I'm frightened of.

A gunshot rings out and a groan sounds from behind me. I don't have time to turn to see, Granda's hand pushes against my back. "Move now," he roars, his anger at full force. "Girls, get to the fucking safe room, now."

Jade pulls on my hand, tugging me along with her as more shots sound. A scream is lodged in my throat as Boz hits the ground, blood soaks through his back, but I'm unable to stop and help, make sure he's okay, Jade's still tugging me along with her, trying to pull me to safety.

The gunshots are relentless, tears fall freely down my face as Finn pushes me and Jade behind him, it's in that moment that I see Granda's down, he's not moving, I can't see his face and I don't want to. My legs buckle beneath me as I see the bullet wound in the back of his head.

My hand claws at my throat as I realise why he's unmoving. God. No. please no.

"Jade, take Holly and go to the safe room," Finn clips out, he's still all business.

"What about you?" Jade asks, and I'm grateful, I'm not able to speak right now. It's utter carnage around us, the men are sprawled on the floor, each one of them having been shot and I'm praying none of them are fatal.

"Go," he yells as yet more bullets start to spray.

"Finn," I scream as he goes down. "No," I can't help it, I sink to the ground and put my hand over his gut wound. Needing to stop the bleeding, wanting to help.

"Go..." he says, his voice weak as his body trembles.

"No, I can't, please don't make me," I plead with him, tears soaking my face. This is too fucking much.

"Jade," Finn groans.

Jade pulls at my arm, "Come on, Hol, we'll get to the

safe room and we'll call for help. Please," now she's the one pleading with me, but she, unlike me, hasn't broken down, she's all business.

I let her pull me to my feet and notice the gun in her hand.

"Take another step and I'll shoot him dead," a male voice calls out and I turn to see a balding guy step forward, gun in hand pointed at Finn.

I stand stock still, unable to move. My throat lodged with fear as my tears continue to cascade down my face.

"Go," Finn urges us, but neither Jade nor I can.

"Ms. Gallagher, you're coming with us," the arsehole demands.

"She's not going anywhere," Jade yells, her gun pointed at the man and she fires. I watch with absolute horror as the man falls to his knees, blood pouring from the wound in his chest.

The sound of footsteps has me backing up a step, the man on his knees lifts his gun and takes aim once again. Gunshots sound and pain slices through my shoulder. I release a strangled cry as more shots sound, this time when fire and pain throb from my leg, I collapse to the ground, my head connecting with the steps with a jarring thud. Blackness seeps into my vision, the pain in my body intensifies and the last conscious thought I have is that I didn't hear a sound from Jade.

EIGHTEEN

ROMERO

"Antonio..." Dante says with a nod of his head. "It's good to see you."

Our cousin flashes us his easy smile, "Same, although, I'm pissed no one thought to inform me of what happened the last time you were here."

My teeth clench at his words. The last time we were here was a few days ago when Holly was shot. The image of her laying on the ground bleeding is something that repeats over and over in my mind. I don't think I'll ever not be able to see it. I should have protected her.

Antonio Conti is the head of the Conti family. His mother and our father were siblings. Antonio's father, mother, sister-in-law, and nephew were slaughtered at the hands of their enemy - the Romano's. When that happened, we, the Famiglia, went to war and wiped out the Romano's. Of course, they're not all gone. There's two that remain Stefano and Fabio. The uncle and nephew duo are the worst of the Romano's but went into hiding when our family went on a rampage.

"Well, you were..." Dante begins, "pre-occupied and we needed to get Holly home."

He nods, "I understand," he turns to me, "your wife is very beautiful and probably one of the smartest women I've met. She takes no shit from anyone and that includes Luca."

Luca Conti is the coldest motherfucker I have ever met. He was in love with Aurora Romano when he was a teenager, he watched as her car got blown to pieces with her inside, not to mention he saw his parents and nephew dead. He changed, as would any of us, he's the most feared man in Illinois. But he's also one of the most loyal men I've ever encountered and would do anything for his family. That includes Dante, Alessio, and I.

I smile as Dante smirks. "That's Holly, she also has a mean right hook." Antonio grins, eager to learn more. "Georgina showed up the next morning and Holly had enough of her shit."

Antonio rubs his hands together. "I need to know, Fratello, where are you finding these women?"

"Ireland," Dante replies dryly, which has Antonio throwing his head back and laughing. The ass.

The door opens behind us and in walks, Luca, Marco, Enzo, Dominic, Manny, and Giovanni. "Well now, I had no idea we were having a party," Enzo says as he takes in Dante and I.

The Conti brothers are close, as I am with Dante. But the seven of them have managed to integrate into society more than most Mafia families. I suspect that's down to Marco, who studied law at his father's insistence, hoping it would make the family seem more respectable. The rest of the brother's own multiple businesses. They have the biggest front than any other outfit.

Antonio ignores his brother. "So, what brings you

here?" The brothers are here in New York trying to work out a deal for some real estate.

"Carter," Dante quickly explains all the shit that's happened with Georgina, "how well do you know him?"

Antonio shrugs. "The man's trying to be in everyone's business. He wants to make a name for himself but it's never going to happen. Yes, he's got contacts but they're not the right ones to make moves in this industry. Why?"

"I have a feeling about the man," I say, he's too slick.

Luca nods. "I agree, the man is a fucking sap, yet thinks he's the biggest player in town. Fuck. There's something I do not like about him."

Dante's cell starts ringing and chills run down my spine. I reach into my pocket and pull out my own cell, it's been almost three hours since I left Holly, and I've not heard a fucking thing from her or Finn.

Dante's sharp intake of breath is enough to have my body going solid. "When?" he clips out. "Where?"

I look at him, needing to find out what the fuck is going on.

"We're on our way." He ends the call and turns to me. His face set in stone and I brace knowing whatever the fuck he's going to say isn't going to be good.

"The girls returned home from shopping and were ambushed. Shots fired and men down, I'm not sure who but we're going to the hospital. Now."

I'm already moving toward the door before he even finishes telling me what's happened. Fuck. My guts burning, I knew I shouldn't have left her. My gut is never fucking wrong. Damn it.

"Rome," Dante says, his voice void of emotion, he's trying to calm me. It's not going to work. I'm not going to be calm until she's in my fucking arms.

I slide into the car, Stefan's jaw clenched tight. "Any news?" I demand as soon as Dante's in the vehicle. Adriano puts his foot down and we set off toward the hospital.

"No, nothing. Everyone is on their way, Denis and Liam are pissed, they have no idea what's happened to Holly or Jade."

They're not the only fucking ones.

Anger and worry course through me as I wait for fucking news while trying to get to the hospital. Once again, my wife's life has been put in danger and I'm nowhere fucking near her.

Once we arrive at the hospital, my feet are moving quicker than they have before. Dante keeping pace with me and my gut sinks when we reach the waiting room and see the worry and heartache etched on everyone's face.

Makenna's face is pale, Denis and Danny look as though they're about to tear the motherfucking hospital apart, and Melissa is on her cell talking low.

"Tell us," Dante demands walking toward his wife.

It's Liam that speaks. "Finn and Jade are in surgery. Both have been shot, Finn is critical as he lost a lot of blood and the bullet did some damage." His hands ball into fists. "Seamus was shot in his head, he didn't make it. Neither did Malachy. Boz and Reilly are okay, both have been shot, but will survive."

Fuck. Seamus.

"Where's Holly?" I ask and the whimper that escapes Edwina makes me want to punch someone. "Someone tell me where the fuck my wife is!"

"She's gone. Whoever the fuck shot them, took her. Boz and Reilly have no idea who it was and we have to wait for Finn and Jade to find out more information," Liam tells me.

I blink at the motherfucker. "Want to say that again?" I rumble, hoping he's wrong.

Danny steps forward, his voice low as he tells me. "Boz said she was shot twice and she was taken."

Pain slices through me. She's gone. How the fuck has this happened?

"Rome," Makenna says as she takes a step toward me. "We're going to find her."

I swallow through the rage and despair that's cascading through me. Once again, I've failed, I've let her down.

"What happened?" I bark out, my voice vibrating with anger.

Danny sighs, his hand running through his hair, "From what Lis has managed to find out, as soon as they stepped out of the car they were ambushed," I watch as he swallows hard, trying to fight the emotion etched on his face. "They picked them off one by one. Finn, he tried to protect the girls but he was outgunned and outnumbered."

My fists clenched as I gaze around the room, not one motherfucker can meet my eyes. Denis hasn't lifted his gaze from the floor since I walked in. "What haven't you told me."

"Holly was shot twice, she passed out before they took her," Denis says, tears shining in his eyes. His face filled with pain and anguish. He's lost his father, his brother's in surgery as is his cousin and his daughter is missing.

My knees threaten to buckle beneath me. "Tell me you have something," I plead. Needing to find out where the fuck my wife is.

"I'm trying, Romero, I really am, whoever took her was good. Every fucking camera feed in and around Makenna's house was hacked, and put on a loop. The same feed over and over again. I'm not giving up, I'm going to find her,"

Melissa vows and she once again goes back to her cell phone where she's typing furiously.

"It has to be those fucking Russians," I snarl. It's the only motherfucking thing that makes sense. Right now, we have no issue with anyone else. We've managed to forge a path where we're on top and anyone wanting to make a name for themselves will be known. There are no unknowns in town, no one has tried to worm their way in.

Dante's eyes are hard, his jaw clenched. "Then it's time we showed those fuckers what happens when you mess with us."

Both Denis and Danny step forward, their eyes filled with determination. "Strength in numbers," Danny says, his gaze on Melissa, "you find anything, let us know."

She nods, her mouth set into a tight line.

"We're going to make a statement. One that can't be fucking missed. It's going to be hard, bloody, and messy."

Liam and Hayden step forward. "Let's make the city bleed," Liam announces, the grin he has is sadistic, no doubt wanting revenge for his daughter being shot.

Dante and I walk ahead of the Irish men, Liam and Danny on their phones calling for backup. "Where the fuck is Alessio?" I demand to know, I'm barely keeping my shit contained and my brother isn't here.

"I have no fucking idea. I've called him three times and no answer. When I get my hands on him, I'm going to kill him," Dante growls, rightfully pissed. Alessio is Dante's Consigliere, he's to be on hand at any moment. But Alessio's not beating to anyone's drum but his own and he's looking to get himself killed.

"Get in line, brother, the way I'm feeling, I'm taking everyone out."

"That's what love will do for you," he says and my body

goes solid. "Come on, Rome, you can't hide it any longer. We all know you love Holly, it's clear as fucking day."

"Love," I scoff, that's an emotion I have no grasp of.

He glances at me and shakes his head, not saying a word until we're sliding into the front seat of the car having given out orders - we're to go in hot, with as many men as possible. The Irish men getting into their own cars, we're all anxious, and pissed.

"Loving someone isn't a weakness, Rome," Dante tells me, his hands gripping the steering wheel tightly. "It's a fucking strength. Loving Makenna doesn't mean I'm weak, it makes me fucking invincible. That feeling you have running through you. The one where you want to tear apart the world and get your wife back. That's what being in love is. You'd do anything to protect them, cherish them...."

Love them.

Fuck. he's right. I'd do all of that and more for Holly.

"Loving someone is putting them first. Wanting them to be happy, doing everything in your power to make them so."

I grit my teeth. A piercing pain lances through my chest.

"Loving Holly is what makes you a better man."

Damn it.

How the fuck did I not realize that I loved her?

"I can't breathe," I tell him, for the first time in my life, I'm showing my brother my weakness.

He nods. "I can't imagine what you're going through, Rome, but we're going to get her back," he vows. "That feeling you have. Hold onto it. She's going to need you to have it. Use it against those who have harmed her."

The heaviness I have in my chest is making it hard to focus. It's a reminder of what's missing, what I failed to protect. Fuck. She's my wife. The only person in this world

I cherish above all else. The one woman I'd happily walk away from the family for. My lifeline.

The rest of the car journey is silent, both of us lost in our thoughts. I can't think about anything other than Holly. That may make me selfish, I don't give a fuck. She's mine. I'd tear down the fucking white house if that's where she was being held.

Dante stops outside a boxing gym; I turn to him in question. "What the fuck are we doing here?"

He smirks. "This is Maksim's pride and joy. He has the biggest and best fighters in the States. He prides himself on how nothing touches this business. Well, that's about to change." He slides out of the car and I'm right behind him.

Maksim doesn't want his boxing empire mixing with his organized crime? Well too fucking bad. I reach behind me to my back hostler, my fingers closing around the butt of my gun. Just having the weight of it in my hands makes me feel a little less frantic. I know I'm a little feral right now. I couldn't give a fuck. That's what happens when you take a man's woman. When you take a good fucking woman. One that's so pure she breathes life into a dead man and that's exactly what I was until she came into my life.

I existed, I breathed, slept, and worked. I didn't live. I went through the motions, did what was expected of me. I didn't feel. Until Holly. Now, well now I'm feeling too fucking much. The pain of losing her almost brought me to my knees.

Doors slam closed and I know we're being surrounded by our men, by the Irish men.

Dante raises his hand, stopping anyone from going in ahead. "I don't give a fuck what you do. Shoot to kill if you have too. Leave at least two alive."

The men nod in agreement, each of them wearing the

same expression on their faces. Anger, determination, and vengeance. The Irish want revenge for the bastards taking their princess. The Italian's want revenge for them taking my wife. We're all united in one cause. Getting Holly back and making the fuckers pay for taking her.

We breach the gym, and I don't even hesitate, my gun is aimed and I shoot. One after one, the Russian men fall. I don't stop until every bullet is emptied from my magazine.

"We had a truce," Maksim roars as he steps into the chaos.

Dante once again raises his hand, stopping the onslaught. "We did, so want to tell me why your men ambushed my family? Why your men killed mine and took my sister-in-law?"

The blank expression on the bastard's face makes me want to lunge at him. To take my knife and peel strips of skin from his face. I want the fucker to scream and beg for his life as I bleed his life from him.

"My men did no such thing," he replies, his voice void of emotion. For a man that's lost men here, he's acting like it doesn't faze him.

"Lies!" Dante sneers at him, "who else would be so fucking bold and do this?"

Maksim glances at me. "Word on the street is, someone isn't happy you found a wife."

I narrow my eyes at him, "Really? And what exactly have you heard?"

I'm ready to fucking throw my knife at him, wanting it to pierce his skin and stick into his heart.

"Now, Romero, surely you are not that stupid? I detest this game. I do not like to state the obvious. A woman scorned is a crazy woman. But add in who her family is, and you have a murderous crazy woman."

I turn my gaze to Stefan. "Find Carter," I demand. "I want to know where that fucking cunt is."

He nods and turns on his heel, his cell to his ear as he moves past the throngs of men and outside.

"I find out you're lying, Maksim, and you'll have a lot more to worry about than your gym," Dante informs him, "What happened here, this is only the beginning, you do not come after my family."

Before Maksim can retort, the door behind him opens and out walks my fucking brother.

The sharp intakes of breaths from our men tells me there's no way he can be dealt with by Dante and me. He's shown that he's betrayed the family, and there's no escaping what's coming his way.

"Boss," Stefan says, "Danny's wife has called, she and your wife have the bitch," the smile on his face is reflected on every other man's face.

"Let's go," Dante snaps. "Alessio, you too." There's no mistaking his tone.

Alessio has fucked up and he'll be punished. But right now, our focus is on Holly.

NINETEEN
HOLLY

I blink as I try to fight the darkness once again. My shoulder and leg are burning with pain, every move I make has me biting down on my lip to stop the whimpers or cries from escaping me. I'm not sure how long I've been here, probably a few hours.

I've no idea how we got here, or where here even is. I woke up tied to this chair. My arm pulled behind my back, making the wound at my shoulder hurt. I'm shrouded in darkness; the only light is dim and it's coming from the two small windows on either side of this room.

No one has come since I woke up, I'm wondering if they'll even bother coming back, or will they let me die here. The wound to my leg is worse than the one on my shoulder. The bleeding has slowed, I can feel that they've bandaged it up somewhat. But when I move my leg, I can feel the warmth of the blood running down my leg.

The door opens and the lights are flicked on, and suddenly I'm blinking harshly for a whole other reason. The blinding lights are too much for my eyes, too powerful for me and my head begins to pound. I try to focus on the bodies moving toward me, but I can't. My vision swims as I try to keep my head up.

"Ms. Gallagher, so nice to see you awake," the man says to me as he steps into my view. His accent is hard to place. I suck in a sharp breath as I refocus my gaze. I can finally see the man, he's short, hell probably only a couple of inches taller than Lis, and she's tiny. He's got a jagged scar which goes from his right eyebrow to his nostril, as well as a scar on his upper lip.

"Do you know who I am?" he questions, his voice holds an air of authority about it.

I blink, I've never seen this man in my life. How the hell should I know who he is?

He steps forward with a smirk playing on his lips, his eyes filled with amusement. I don't see it coming, so I'm unable to brace. He lifts his hand and savagely backhands me. Once again, my vision swims, the blackness creeping into my eyes.

"Now, Ms. Gallagher, I asked you a question..." his tone filled with anger and loathing.

"Bianchi," I spit at him, tasting blood on my lips.

He stills, his entire body going solid. "What did you just say?"

"Bianchi. My name is Holly Bianchi." I know he can hear the pride in my voice.

I'm proud of my husband. I'll never hide who I am, who I'm married too. People may think Romero is a monster, and he very well can be, but to me he's nothing but Rome. My Rome. My safe haven.

The dickhead shakes his head. "No, you're Holly Gallagher." His accent is thicker and that's when I'm able to place it, he's Latino.

I resist the urge to roll my eyes, knowing it'll only cause

me pain. "That is my maiden name. I got married. I'm sorry, it seems as though your invite was somehow lost in the mail," I reply, my tone saccharine sweet.

"Married?" he echoes and I'm wondering if he's hard of hearing or something?

"Yes, I got married, you know, in a church in front of hundreds of guests. The white dress, the veil, the I do's."

"Who?" he snarls at me. He's once again edging closer to me.

I blink at his gruff tone. "Romero Bianchi."

"Fuck!" he roars, the sound reverberating around the room. "That motherfucking bitch."

I frown as ice crawls through my veins. The vibe in the room has changed, it's more volatile, more dangerous, deadlier than before.

"Seems, Mrs. Bianchi, we've been stitched up. Had I known you were the wife of that monster, I would not have ordered my men to take you."

I swallow past the fear and ask the question that's on the tip of my tongue. "Who?" It's weak and I hate I'm showing this bastard weakness. "Who stitched us up?" I ask, and I'm pleased this time my voice was stronger, concise, and filled with anger.

His eyes narrow. "Pussy is only good when the woman is soft and sweet to the outside world but a whore between the sheets. Pussy that's filled with venom on the outside and used between the sheets is fucking useless. That motherfucking bitch played me like a fiddle."

Whoops, seems as though someone needs to try a dating site.

"She hates you; I'm wondering what you did to piss her off," he shakes his head in disgust. "Crossing her isn't the smartest move."

"If I knew who she was, I'd be able to answer that for you," I reply sarcastically, I'm not even sure if he's talking to me or himself.

He grins at me and it's sadistic and I can imagine how merciless he can be. "Georgina," he informs me, laughter echoing through his voice.

Fucking bitch.

"What does it feel like?" I ask, unable to stop the words from tumbling out. "Knowing you're going to die? I mean, you've not only pissed off the Irish Mafia, which by the way, was a stupid move. My family has anger issues on their best days, piss them off and you're asking for it. But also, to piss off the Italian's. You must have some serious balls, or Georgina's got you wrapped around her finger."

He releases a low growl, this time when he steps forward, it's not to backhand me, but to viciously throw his fist into my face. My nose crunches beneath the blow as blood instantly flows from my nostrils.

Fuck. He's broken it.

Tears sting my eyes at the pain.

"Shut up," he snarls. "Shut the fuck up and let me think."

I do as he says, the blood continues to flow down my face.

"What did you do to her?" he asks and I'm getting whiplash from him. One minute he's angry, the next curious. He needs to make up his damn mind.

"I married a man she used to fuck. One who has continued to rebuff her cheap arse ever since." God, she's fucking desperate.

"She's been trying to fuck that Italian asshole?" he questions as he begins to pace.

"Yes, she even slept with his brother the other night hoping to make him jealous."

His swift intake of breath is enough to have me brace for the onslaught of what's to come. Once again, his fist plows into my face. "I'm fucked either way," he says as he lands a blow to my midsection, taking the wind from me. "I'm going to die. There's no way your family will let me live. I may as well make it worthwhile."

My heart sinks at his words. He's going to kill me.

I pray when it's all over, Romero will be okay, and he'll learn to love.

The darkness takes me once again as the man lands a punch to my temple.

TWENTY

ROMERO

"Get the fuck into the car Alessio," Dante's tone is menacing, it's one he's never used on us before, it's his boss' voice.

Our brother glares at him but does as he's told, knowing Dante's not messing around right now. Ales is close to death; the smell lingers in the air. He had better have a fucking good explanation as to why he's in the office of the Russian bastard.

Dante slides into the driver's side and I into the passenger's side. As soon as the doors are closed, Dante lets loose.

"You have until we get to Makenna and Melissa to explain what the fuck you are doing with the Russian's. I cannot save you from this. Every man has seen the betrayal you have brought to this family by being in that fucking gym."

Alessio fucking sighs, as though what Dante's saying is tiring. "Look, when Dad was alive, I had a job to do, one I'm still doing."

I shake my head, my fists clenched. The rage that's burning through me is butting against me to be let loose.

"That's not how this works, Ales, you start fucking talking and do not leave a single fucking detail out."

"What the fuck?" He grunts.

I glance at Dante, trying to convey with him that he'd better sort him out otherwise I'm going to lose my shit.

"Ales, something you seem not to have grasped right now is, Rome and I are fucking close to putting a bullet in you, we'd do it without remorse. Today is not the motherfucking day to run your mouth and dish out the attitude. Holly's gone. Seamus is dead, and everyone who was with them is currently in hospital, dead, or in surgery. So, start fucking talking."

His sharp intake of breath doesn't help the situation. "Fuck. What happened?"

Now I'm done.

"Not in the mood to enlighten you on what went down. What I want to know is why the fuck you were with the Russians and Alessio, don't piss me off anymore with the lack of details."

"Fuck," he groans. "Dad was deep in bed with the Russians: Drugs, guns, women, you name it, Dad was deeply involved in as were the Russians. Dad believed someone was stealing drugs from him, he wasn't sure if it was the Russian's or the Latinos. I was tasked with getting close to the Russians, to watch over them and report back."

Dante's grip tightens on the steering wheel. "Did you find out if it was them?"

"From what I can tell, they don't fuck around with the drugs. While it's a huge revenue for them, it's not their biggest. They fuck over their partners in the trafficking gig they have going on. They sell women on the side, pretending that they didn't get their quota of women. They also, mark down the price of what they sold for. We're talking five hundred thousand dollars they're pocketing, per woman. But as for the drugs, they don't fuck around with that shit," he tells us, his voice tight and filled with anxiousness.

"Dad's dead, has been for a fucking while now, so why are you still in bed with the fuckers?" I ask, needing to fucking understand why he's betraying us.

"To get close to them, I found a way in. Yelena. She's Maksim's granddaughter." The softness of his voice when he talks about the woman has me tensing. Fuck. "Yelena, she's mine."

"You fell for her? Fucking hell, Ales," Dante gripes, "what the fuck were you thinking?"

"The reason I was at the gym is because I've not been able to get a hold of her in a few days." He's unable to keep the hurt out of his tone, but I can't bring myself to care right now.

I scoff. "You mean, she's not talking to you since you fucked Georgina."

He groans, "Yeah, I fucked up and she ran."

"You shouldn't have fucking gotten so deep with her," Dante snaps. "What the fuck were you thinking?"

"I made mistakes, I'm only fucking human," he fires back, the anger pouring out of him is palpable.

"What the ever loving fuck?" I snarl, pissed that he's getting fucking mad. He's the one who messed up, not us. I turn so I'm facing him, he's glaring at the back of Dante's head. "What's your problem, Ales? Spit it out, and do it quickly. I have to deal with this before I go and find my wife. I'd like to know that you're on my side, I don't want to have to watch my back as I go."

His eyes widen as he rears back. "You'd think I'd betray you?"

"What the fuck do you think the men are thinking right now? You cozying up to the Pakhan of the Bratva?" Not to mention everything he's done to bring harm to Holly, including sleeping with that motherfucking bitch, Georgina.

His jaw clenches. "I'm not cozying up to anyone."

"What's your problem?" I ask again, annoyed at having this fucking discussion. It should have been curbed until I had Holly back. "Is it Dante?"

He sighs. "I don't have a problem with Dante. I have a problem with this whole fucking system. I've worked hard to be a part of the Famiglia, I earned my stripes just as Romero has done and yet, I'm treated as the kid brother. I'm thought of as a pain in the ass. Then when I'm doing what I've been tasked to do, I'm seen as the fucking enemy." His nostrils flare as his face flames with anger.

Dante's jaw clicks, he's about as pissed as I am. Yeah, our wives need us and we're here having this ridiculous conversation.

"You were given the title and role of Consigliere, that's a motherfucking honor. One that you should have grasped and held onto tight. With this shit you've pulled, you don't deserve it."

We're getting closer to Dante and Makenna's house and it's time to wrap this shit up.

"What you proved by your fucking stunt, is that you cannot be trusted. You are not for the family. You are all about you. We grew up, fast and hard, we had too, it was the way things were, but the three of us, we were each other's protectors and Ales, the moment you stopped being that, you became the enemy."

Dante pulls into the drive and I don't hang around to hear Alessio's response. I exit the car, I hear footsteps and car doors slamming shut behind me, the rest of the men have arrived. Good. It's time to get down to business, find out where Holly is and end everyone who harmed her.

Walking into the house, a high pitched screech reaches my ears, I smirk when I realize who that screech belongs to —Georgina. I follow the sound to the basement and to my utter annoyance and astonishment, both Makenna and Melissa have Georgina strapped to a chair, her hair now shaved, giving her a buzz cut and both my sisters-in-law are smiling brightly.

"Ah, Romero," Makenna says happily, but I see the pain behind the facade. She's lost her father. "I'm not sure if you'd recognize Georgina here, but she wasn't being very forthcoming with the information I needed, so Lissa and I decided we'd get her to talk."

I raise a brow. "By shaving all her hair off?" I can't stop the twitching of my lips. Damn, she's got a big head. The hair Georgina did have, hid the size of it well.

Melissa shakes her head, her thick black hair falling around her face. "No, I need her hair gone so when I begin to scalp the bitch, I'll be able to see what I'm doing. Having her lose all her hair is a bonus."

My body goes solid. Did she say scalp? What the fuck? How the hell would she even know about scalping someone?

"You wouldn't dare," Georgina spits. "Do you know who my family is?"

Makenna laughs. "Oh, delusional little girl," she tuts, and I'm pretty sure Georgina is older than both Makenna and Melissa. "Your family is no one of importance. They do not run this world. Hell, they don't even run the fucking street their business is on. I do, my husband does. Us alone. Now, while Lissa here gets set up, we're going to have a little talk."

Georgina snarls at her, her lips twisted into a sneer as her eyes flash fire. "Fuck you, you fucking bitch."

Makenna smiles at her words. "You do not want to piss me off, Georgie Porgie."

Georgina snarls at her. "Don't fucking call me that," she spits out.

Makenna throws her head back and laughs. "Did I hit a nerve? Kids can be awful."

I stand against the wall with my arms crossed over my chest and get ready to watch the show, Melissa's lined up a scalpel, scissors, and gauzes on a wheelie tray, where she got them from, I have no fucking idea, but Melissa's smart as hell, she's also slightly crazy.

"So, where's Holly?" Makenna asks again, she's met with defiance from Georgina. "That's okay, Georgie Porgie, we can wait. Lis here is almost ready for you anyway." Makenna smiles as she lands a harsh punch to Georgina's side.

"You motherfucking bitch!" Georgina wheezes out.

Melissa tuts. "Such an angry little fucking cunt," the way she says cunt is as though she's talking normally to her. "I'd advise you to be as still as you can, one slip and this scalpel is going to do a lot more damage than I intend and that'll piss me off." She sits on the stall that's directly behind Georgina's chair and reaches for the scalpel that's beside her.

"I'll hold her head," Makenna says with a grin and I swear these two are fucking getting a kick out of this shit. "We wouldn't want her to make any sudden movement that would end our fun way too soon."

"Are we supposed to sit back and let this play out?" Danny grumbles, no doubt not wanting his wife in the midst of this.

"That's exactly what we're going to do." Dante grins. "Our wives are bloodthirsty, they've lost Seamus, and Holly's missing; they need to do this and they know when we find Holly's location neither of them are going to be allowed to come with us."

I watch in sick fascination as Makenna holds Georgina's head as Melissa begins to cut along her scalp. Blood trickles down her face with each slice that Melissa inflicts on her. The only noise which can be heard is Georgina's whimpering.

"I have no problem doing this all fucking day," Melissa begins, her tone filled with anger. "Where the fuck is Holly?"

"I don't know!" Georgina cries.

"Bullshit. I saw the men who took her. I also know that they're in close allegiance with your uncle. There's only one reason as to why they'd take her and that's you." Melissa doesn't miss a beat, she continues to cut into her head, following along the edge of her scalp, Georgina's a fucking mess, blood pours from her head like a flowing river.

"Keep lying, Georgina, we've no problem in making things worse for you. This is only the beginning, once Melissa has taken your scalp, it's my turn, and I'll be removing your digits. Then we'll start sending pieces to your family. Which do you think would rile them up the most? Your fingers, toes, or scalp?"

Melissa snickers. "I personally say the scalp. It's so cliche to send a finger."

I'm fucking grateful my wife isn't a fucking crazy bitch. These two are fucking psychos.

"We're not going to kill you." Georgina stills even more at Melissa's words. "Oh no, that would be too fucking easy. See, people like you, Georgina, love the way they look, use it to get what they want." The chuckle that leaves Melissa is sadistic. "What are you going to do when those looks are gone?"

"Please." The fucking bitch whines and pleads. "I'll tell you, I will." Tears and blood soak her face as her gaze finds mine. "This is all your fault. You were mine."

Red hot rage fills me, but I beat it back. I can't do anything yet. I need this bitch to talk. I need to find out where my wife is.

"Where's Holly," Makenna demands, as Melissa moves to where Georgina's ear is, she's still being precise with her incisions. I've never seen anyone be scalped before, but I'd have thought it hurt a fuck of a lot and judging by the pain etched in Georgina's eyes as well as the tears streaming down her face, I'd say my guess was right. I'm glad the fucking cunt's in pain. If I had my way, she'd be in a world of it by the time I was finished with her.

She rattles off the address of a building downtown. "She'll be dead before you even get there." She sneers with glee before letting out a pained cry.

"Oops, that went in a little deeper than I had expected. Oh well," Melissa grins.

"Who's got her?" Makenna asks, her entire body strung tightly, her voice vibrating with anger.

"Jose Ortega." Georgina's grin is wicked, one that claims victory.

Jose Ortega is the head of the Mexican organized crime family. They're not Mafia, more drug dealers, and they also deal in selling women. I wouldn't be surprised if they worked alongside the Russians.

"He's going to have fun with her before he kills her." The bitch laughs.

Fuck that. No one is touching my wife.

I'm over to her in seconds, my hands wrapping around her throat. "If she's not there, I'm going to take my fucking time as I drain your body of blood, I'm going to enjoy watching as the life leaves your eyes."

Fear seeps into her features. Good. Fucking bitch.

"You were meant to be mine," she whimpers, "you loved me."

"No bitch, the only thing I liked was that you knew how to give head. That is it. You're fucking useless. No one wants a used bitch for their wife." My words are harsh, but I don't care, she's brought this on herself. Going after Holly was a sure-fire way to cement her death.

"Why would anyone want you..." Makenna asks, "when they have Holly?"

"You," Melissa begins, waiting patiently to finish what she started, "are like a chuck steak, cheap, easy, and quick. Holly on the other hand is like a filet mignon. Tender, beautiful, and perfection."

Now ain't that the motherfucking truth.

"No one wants your cheap arse when they can have Holly. You should have moved on and found another man to try and worm your way into his bed. But instead, you chose to pursue a married man. You are what gives women a bad name." Melissa looks at me. "You done with her now?"

I smile, she's fucking bloodthirsty. "Sure, try to keep her alive, though. Just in case she's fucking with us."

Melissa fucking salutes me. "No worries, Romero, for what Kenna and I have planned for her, we need her alive and kicking."

I chuckle as I turn away, knowing the women have her

in hand and if she's lying and Holly isn't where she said, well then, it'll be my turn to fucking play with her.

I nod toward Dante and move out of the basement, I hear him barking orders, making sure the women aren't left alone. We won't be making that mistake again. This time there'll be enough guards on them to ensure they're safe. Especially with Makenna being pregnant.

"I'm coming," Ales says, catching up to me.

I don't even glance at him, I don't want him around me right now. While I understand he had a job to do, I don't believe the way he went about it was the right way to do it. He should have told us, Dante especially, seeing as he's now the boss.

"We'll get her back," he tells me, and I ignore him, right now I need to focus all my energy into Holly and making sure we find her.

"I'm driving," Stefan announces, "We're taking the escalade, we need to be inconspicuous."

I nod, whatever, I need to be leaving now.

My breathing starts to shallow as I slide into the vehicle. My thoughts run wild with the things that Ortega could be doing to my wife. I know who he is, I've heard the rumors. That he rapes and murders women who disobey him. He hurts the women who talk back, who want more than being either trafficked or becoming a prostitute for him.

Dante sits beside me, as always, he's sat up straight, facing forward, "We're going to make sure the Ortega men bleed out on the streets." It's a vow and I know my brother, he'd do whatever he can to make sure my wife is protected, and I have men at my back willing to do the same.

I take a steadying breath. I'm going to get my wife back and I'm going to give her the vengeance she needs, that's all the Gallagher's need.

We're going into enemy territory and I'm bringing them a motherfucking war.

TWENTY-ONE
ROMERO

There are seven cars in this convoy. Each of them holding at least four men. There's already three at the location Georgina disclosed as to where Jose is holding Holly. Not to mention two more on the way with the weapons we'll be needing.

"We'll be going in hot," Dante announces, his tone clear and concise, he's on a conference call right now with the other men, each of them ready in case there's an ambush.

The Ortega men must know we're coming. Surely, they'd realize I'd do whatever it took to get my wife back. That I'd hunt, maim, and kill anyone who was involved in her abduction.

"Boss, there's seven guards outside the house, there's also two vehicles doing checks around the block. Then there's two men sitting in the opposite house keeping a lookout." Lewis informs us, he's one of Makenna's men, he's Finn's right hand man and is pissed his friend is lying in hospital due to these fuckers.

My gut clenches with anticipation. We're definitely on

the way to the right house. There's no way they'd have that much manpower if they weren't hiding her.

"Christian, I want you, Danilo, and Alfonso, to take out the cars. I don't care how you do it. I want them to stop circling the block," Dante instructs, "Alex," My body tenses at that motherfucker's name. I haven't seen him since he made a pass at Holly, he's lucky he's still breathing. "I want you and Lorenzo to take out those guards across the street."

"On it, boss," Alex replies, no doubt sucking up, the fucking ass.

"Lewis, can you and your men get rid of the seven-foot guards?" Dante inquires and I'm getting antsy; it's been hours since Holly's been taken and as we draw closer, the pain of losing her pierces my chest like a fucking needle.

"Yes, and we'll do it silently. No one will suspect we're coming." I can hear the glee in his voice. This is what the men are waiting for, to unleash the anger that's running through them.

The Irish lost two good men today, one, their boss, the other a soldier. They also feel deeply that an Underboss as well as a fucking princess are fighting for their lives in the hospital. And the Italian's are joining them in the rage because my wife has been taken and the Irish because the granddaughter and niece of the bosses has been shot and kidnapped.

"We're seven minutes out," Stefan declares and a calm washes over me. This is what I do, what I live for. I'm the man that doesn't allow emotion to lead him. Right now, I push aside the rage that's taken a hold of me since I found out that not only was my wife fucking kidnapped but also shot.

"You good?" Dante asks, his gaze searching my face.

I sense what he means is, *"if you're not good, you're*

staying back." They can't afford a liability and if I let my emotions get the best of me, that's what I'll be. If he thought I wasn't good, he'd lock me down and make sure I wasn't anywhere near the action.

"I'm good," I assure him.

He stares at me for a beat and then nods. "Good, we're almost there. You're to go in and go to Holly," he instructs.

I bite back the urge to lash out. "With all due respect, Dante, that isn't going to happen. You know it and I know it. Denis' main concern will be Holly, mine is too, but I also need to make sure Ortega doesn't hurt her again. Don't fucking ask me to be something I'm not."

The urge to kill the motherfucker is riding me hard. I've never been a man to hide from confrontation and I've always been fiercely protective of my family. Whatever the fuck Dante got into his head, he needs to get it out. I'll be getting my revenge. No one takes my wife. Hell, no one fucking hurts my wife and lives to tell the tale.

Dante's eyes harden but he nods stiffly. If the tables were turned, there'd be no way in hell anyone would be able to hold him back. He'd be the first one into the fucking house, gutting everyone who stands between him and Ortega.

The car slowly creeps up to the house, the convoy right behind us. "Let's go," Dante says and within seconds everyone is exiting their vehicles. The men are there handing out weapons and pushing us toward the house.

Dante's to my right, Ales to my left, with Danny, Denis, and Liam bringing up my rear. Cian and Patrick are breaching from the rear with their man at their backs. There's almost fifty of us entering this house and none of us could give a fuck who's caught in the crossfire. This is what happens when you fuck with us.

Shots are fired before I even enter the house, the rapid gunfire echoes into the night. I follow the sound of the footsteps, hearing the men shout clear as they move through each room. "Found her," I hear yelled, unsure who it's coming from.

I break into a sprint, pushing past everyone who stands in my way. The fury I have burns through my lungs as I move toward the room which holds my wife. As soon as I enter the room, I take in every single piece of it in a sweeping glance. The blood that's scattered along the floor, the men who are hanging their heads in shame, all of them having guns pointed at them. I breathe in the metallic scent of blood. I know instantly that it belongs to Holly.

When my gaze lands on her, my heart fucking shatters. I'm glued to the spot, unable to move. The sight of her tears at me. Her head is drooped down, she's unmoving, and blood completely surrounds her at her feet. Denis reaches her before I do, his touch gentle as he tries to move her. That's when I get a look at her face. My beautiful wife, so full of love and life, is unconscious. Her face is battered with bruises, blood splattered across it. She looks as though she's in a fucking horror movie.

I hear laughter and turn my head away from Holly to find Jose Ortega laughing like a fucking maniac.

Pain, anger, and worry rush through me. I want to go to her, but I can't. Not yet. I need this motherfucker to hurt, to bleed for what he's done to her.

I try to tamper down the urge and push past my gut instinct to go to her, to take her into my arms and hold her against me. I've never felt this way before. So, fucking gutted. I never thought I'd ever love someone but seeing Holly so broken, beaten, and fragile, makes me realize just how much I love her. How much I failed her. She deserves better than what I have given her.

Alessio moves and pins the fucker to the wall. Whispering something in his ear.

"I'm taking her to the hospital, as soon as she's checked in, I'll be back," Denis says, his jaw clenched tight, his eyes narrowed in on the motherfucking bastard. "You handling him here?"

I shake my head. "No, I'll have Stefan bring you to where we're going." We need to get out of here before the cops arrive. All the gunshots in this side of town wouldn't usually raise too many brows, it'll take the cops a while to arrive, but the calls that'll come in, telling them about the amount of foot activity that's going on, could lead to them coming sooner rather than later.

"I'll be there, he deserves everything that's coming to him." I see the unshed tears in Denis's eyes.

This wasn't meant to happen. Our women don't get hurt. We keep them out of the family. They're to be revered, protected, loved. Yet, here we are, a bleeding and beaten Holly. He'll pay and when he does, it's going to be painful.

I'll repay him in kind. For every injury he inflicted on my wife, he'll receive the same. Only worse.

"Alessio, time to move. You'll ride with the bastard," Dante announces, and I see the men stand a little taller, they're not happy with it and I can't blame them. But this is Dante giving Ales a way to make things right, or at least to make some amends.

Danny, Hayden, and Liam are moving Holly out of the house. Danny has her wrapped up in his arms. Her head pressed against his chest as he cradles her. I should be doing that, but I'm still rooted to the spot. My heart pounds a mile a minute.

"Are you coming?" Denis asks me softly. The man is close to the edge. I know the feeling. I never thought I'd be in this position and yet here I am, feeling every fucking emotion under the sun and having no idea how to deal with it.

"Go," Dante says. "The men will sit on him. He'll not be touched until we come back. You need to make sure she's okay."

I don't want the fucker to be alive when she wakes up. Having her know that he's dead will put her mind at ease, knowing he can't hurt her again. But Dante's right. I don't fucking like it, but I need to see her. I need to know she's going to pull through. I have to hear everything that the bastard did to her.

I nod, unable to speak right now, not trusting myself even if I could.

Denis slaps me on the back. "You'll be the one she'll want to see," he says as hurt flashes through his eyes. "It pains me to fucking say this, but it's the truth. When you have a daughter, you'll know exactly what I'm feeling. But I couldn't have asked for a better man for my daughter, Romero. That's the God's honest truth. I know you'll get revenge for what that fucker did to our Holly, I know you'll unleash that monster that's so close to the surface. When you do, I'll be standing on the sideline fucking cheering you on."

That has me looking over at him. "You'll stand back and let me do it?" If that was my child, I would by vying for blood, fuck what anyone else thought.

"Oh, I'll get in my own fucking punches but you," he shakes his head. "You'd off anyone who took the privilege of killing him away from you."

Fuck. He's right, I would.

"It's time to go," Dante urges us, and I nod, following him out of this fucking hell hole and find out if my wife is okay.

EVERYONE IS SITTING in the waiting room, not one of us has moved since Holly was admitted. That was well over two hours ago and I'm losing my goddamn mind with each minute that passes. Denis is pacing and glancing up at the clock every other second. Danny has his head bent and his hands clasped behind his neck, Melissa comforting him with her hand on his thigh. No one is talking, all of us in reflective silence.

Liam, Edwina, and Hayden have been to check in with Jade, she's awake and doing okay. The bullet hit her side but managed to not hit any major organs. She has a few cracked ribs, meaning she'll be in pain for a while, but she'll eventually be okay. She's filled everyone in on what happened once they finished their shopping trip. Finally, everyone was able to hear what went down. Knowing everyone had put their life on the line to save my wife - Jade included is a fucking blessing. I'm in debt to them all and anything they need, I'm there. No fucking questions.

Finn, the man is in critical condition. The gut shot he sustained did hit something vital and the doctors worked on him for fucking hours. They've told Makenna to prepare for the worst, the next twenty-four to forty-eight hours are critical.

When Edwina told Jade that Seamus died, they thought she'd have to be sedated. She was devastated and I can only imagine what Holly's going to be like when she finds out that her Grandfather didn't make it. The man was pronounced DOA, the bullet to the back of the head killed him instantly.

Malachy was shot in the back, it was a through and through, but it went through his heart. He was never going to be able to make it. Both Boz and Reilly are up and moving, they wanted to sit and wait, but Makenna sent them home, told them to rest, that the time will come when we'd all get our revenge. Her words were easy to read, we're all going to war. They're not going to get away with what they have done.

The door opens and a petit doctor stands in the doorway, "I'm looking for a Romero and a Denis?"

I step forward, a lump lodged in my throat. "Holly's awake and is asking to see you both," she tells us with a smile.

"She's okay?" Denis asks, his voice hoarse.

The doctor nods. "She is, she's going to be in pain for a while. Both bullets were through and throughs, whoever bandaged her leg, saved her life."

Fucking bastards.

"She's got a few broken bones along with a lot of swelling and bruising, but she's awake, alert, and asking for her husband and father."

My legs wobble as relief washes through me. She's alive. She's awake. Thank fuck.

"Take me to her," I demand, needing to see her. The doctor nods and instructs Denis and I to follow her.

It doesn't take us long before we're at Holly's room, the doctor pushes the door open, and I reach out for the wall as my knees almost buckle beneath me. She's sitting up, her eyes wide and puffy from the swelling, her nose covered in a bandaged, but my beautiful wife has a small smile on her face. That fucking smile is almost my undoing.

"Doll face," I whisper as I push off the wall, needing that extra boost to get to her.

"Hon," she replies, her voice soft and croaky. "I'm okay," she assures me. "I'm okay." Her hands reach out for me, and I pull her gently into my embrace, burying my face into her neck, breathing her in. "I'm okay," she says once again as a tremor runs through her tiny body.

"I've got you, babe." I promise her, "I'm never letting you out of my sight again."

Her body begins to shake, and I draw her even closer, "I'll be okay with that," she tells me as her tears soak my shirt.

"Baby-girl," Denis says, I release Holly with a kiss to her head and step away from the bed, I don't look at her dad.

I fucking can't. My eyes are stinging with tears and I know by the deepness of his voice he's either crying or close to it. I'll let him have his moment with her. Let him see that she's alive and safe.

When he's done, I'm pulling her into me again. I can't let her go. Frightened that she'll be gone if I don't. I'm a fucking Underboss. We don't get scared of anything. Yet, losing my wife terrifies me.

I finally realize Dante was right. Loving Holly isn't a weakness, it's my ultimate strength. It gives me the power to wipe out gangs and families if need be. I'd do whatever the fuck I have to, gut whoever the hell I have to, as long as she's safe and in my bed.

TWENTY-TWO

HOLLY

The pain throbbing in my head isn't as bad as the excruciating pain coming from both my shoulder and leg. Fuck. I never thought about what it would be like to be shot before, but they don't tell you it hurts like hell.

I see the way Romero and Da are close to losing it. Their eyes, they're filled with darkness, pain and devastation etched on both of their faces.

"I'm okay," I tell them, hoping to ease some of the tension that's in their bodies.

"Doll face," Rome begins, his voice hoarse as though he's close to crying. "You're alive. You're far from fucking okay."

Da nods, "You took years off me, Baby-girl. Years. I thought you were dead sitting in that fucking chair."

"Is Granda okay?" I whisper, as the image of him lying on the ground with a gunshot wound at the back of his head rolls through my mind.

Romero's hand tightens around mine and from that small gesture I already know what the answer will be.

"No, baby-girl, he's not. He didn't make it," Da's gravelly voice tells me how close to the edge he is.

Tears fall from my eyes. It's not fair. We've only just found him, we finally got him in our lives and now he's gone.

"What about Finn?" I ask through the lump in my throat.

"He's hanging in there," Rome says, and I know what he's not saying. Finn may not make it.

"Jade?"

Da pats my hand. "She's okay; she's out of surgery and will be fine."

I'm too afraid to find out about the men that were with us, but I have to know. "What about Malachy, Boz, and Reilly?"

"Boz and Reilly are home, the bullets were through and throughs. Makenna made them go home and rest. I'm sorry, doll face, Malachy didn't make it."

God, why would anyone do this? It makes no bloody sense. I can't wrap my head around the destruction they caused.

I lick my lips as my gaze darts between the two men who mean the most to me in this world. Both of whom have pained expressions on their faces, no doubt from my tears. "Who took me?" I don't know his name; I have no idea who or why he did it.

"He's the head of the Mexican organized crime family. They deal more in drugs than anything else," Da explains.

I frown and pain explodes between my eyes at the movement. God, even moving my brows is painful, that arsehole sure did some damage. "Why? I didn't think either the Irish or the Italian's were at war with them."

I need to understand why this happened.

"That's something we're not entirely sure about. See, neither of us are at war with them, or weren't," Rome tells me, his jaw clenched. "But we do know that he and Georgina were in it together."

My blood runs cold at his words, and then I remember what the man said to me. *"Pussy is only good when the woman is soft and sweet to the outside world but a whore between the sheets. Pussy that's filled with venom on the outside and used between the sheets is fucking useless. That motherfucking bitch played me like a fiddle."*

"He didn't know about you," I tell Rome. "He kept calling me Ms. Gallagher." My voice is shaky as the pain throughout my body intensifies. "When I told him that I was Mrs. Bianchi. He lost his mind. He had no idea we were married. Georgina played him," I explain to them, but neither look like they care. "Is he dead?"

It's Romero that answers, his voice thick with anger and darkness. "Not yet, we needed to be here. Make sure that you're okay."

The blackness is pulling at me as sleep tries to claim me. "Make him pay," I slur as my eyes flutter close.

I hear movement, the scraping of a chair against the floor. Then there's hands on me. A light kiss against my forehead. "Sleep, Baby-girl. I'll be back later," Da promises me and he pulls away from me.

Then Romero's scent fills my nostrils and I inhale it, fighting against the pull to stay awake, to be here with my husband. His hands frame my face, his lips lingering on mine ever so softly.

"I've got you baby. I'm going to make it hurt; I'm going to make him regret hurting you," he vows as he whispers. "No one hurts you."

"Love..." I breathe, "you."

His forehead rests against mine, just as the darkness takes me, the last thing I hear him say is, "I know doll face. I love you too."

GUNSHOTS SOUND and a scream lodges in my throat.

Granda's lying on the ground, a bullet hole in his face, blood seeping out of it. "Hol..." The gurgling sound is too much. I can't help the whimper that escapes me.

"I'm so sorry," I weep, this should have never happened. He should be alive and happy, ready to meet his newest grandchild.

"Ah, Ms. Gallagher," the man sneers as he lifts his gun and aims it at me. The sound of the gunshot is loud and reverberates around my head.

I suck in a deep breath as I lurch forward, my eyes opening widely as I try and fight the pain. It's then I realise I'm in the hospital, the memories return, and sadness hits me deeply, cutting through the pain of my injuries and adding to them.

There's a beeping noise which breaks through the heartache, I glance around the room and see it's the machine I'm hooked up to going crazy. The door opens and a nurse walks in, a beautiful smile on her face.

"Hey, there darlin', are you in pain?"

I nod, unsure if I'm able to speak right now.

"Let me take a look and see if I can help with that." She reaches for my chart and begins to flick through it.

The door opens once again, and I smile when I see Edwina pushing Jade in a wheelchair. "Aww, good, you're awake, I checked in with you earlier, but you were asleep, and I didn't want to disturb you," Edwina tells me as comes to a stop beside my bed.

Jade instantly reaches out and curls her hand around mine. "I was so worried," she tells me, her lips pursed as anger rolls through her eyes.

"I'm okay," I assure her, and I feel as though I'll be saying that for a while now.

The nurse gives me some painkillers and tells me to call her if I need anything.

"I'm going to check in on Finn," Edwina tells us when the nurse leaves, "Makenna's busy now and the guys are with Romero and Denis, I don't want him to wake alone." She quickly gives both Jade and I a kiss on our cheek, "Love you, Hol, I'm so glad you're okay."

I bite my lip to stop the tears from spilling over. "Back at you," I whisper. My heart is so fucking sore right now. We're all feeling the effects of losing Seamus.

He was my Granda, Makenna's Da, Edwina's brother, and Jade's uncle. We loved him dearly and now he's gone. It's too much. We can't grieve. Not yet. There's too much going on for any of us to take a moment and breathe.

"No more bullshit, Holly, how are you feeling?" Jade asks once we're alone.

I sigh. "Honestly? I'm exhausted, I'm sore, and I'm wondering when my husband will be back."

She grins at me. "The pain and exhaustion will go, and when it does, you'll be okay, until then, know your Da, Danny, and Romero are making sure the bastard won't get his hands on you again. As for Makenna and Melissa, well those two little savages are making sure Georgina gets her comeuppance."

I raise a brow. "What do you mean?"

Her grin widens. "Well from what I've heard, before

they found you, Makenna and Melissa managed to find Georgina and proceeded in scalping her."

I blink. "I'm sorry, what?"

Jade giggles. "Yeah, that was my first thought too. But damn, it was fucking genius and to make things worse, as soon as the girls had word that you were found, they left Georgina bleeding and tied up to come be here. Right now, they're finishing what they started."

I narrow my eyes at her little pout. "You're sad you're not there, aren't you?"

She shrugs. "That bitch is the reason Uncle Seamus is dead, why we're all here in this motherfucking hospital, and why we're anxiously awaiting word on whether or not Finn is going to pull through. So, hell yes, I wanted to get my shot in on that bitch."

Not for the first time, I'm wondering how the hell I'm related to these women.

"So, now that we have a moment alone. Are you going to tell me the truth about what went down?"

She closes her eyes. "I should have known you'd not believe the story."

Is she for real? "Jade, firstly, you're more like Melissa than Makenna, you'd use your fists or a knife before you'd reach for a gun. Secondly, you wouldn't be so stupid to be caught with a murder weapon. So, spill it."

She sighs in resignation. "Fine, I didn't kill that stupid bastard. He shot at Hayden and Hayden killed him. But then the cops were coming. It had to have been a set up. I mean, they were practically on us within minutes. So, I did the only thing I could think of, I told Hayden to go."

Realization hits me. "You took the blame for him. Pretended the man shot at you and you accidentally returned fire."

She nods. "I had to. The family is expanding, do you know how hard Hayden's worked to become a captain, how much he wanted that? When he was overlooked for the position, he was gutted. Then he found out he was going to be an Underboss. I couldn't let him go to jail, I just couldn't."

"So, you're looking at doing time now instead."

"Better me than him. If he went to jail, he'd have to work even harder when released to become an Underboss. Not to mention the number of times he's been in trouble with the cops. If he was the one to take the rap, he'd be fucked, Hol, I couldn't do it."

I think about Danny and Mal, and I know I'd do whatever I could to keep them out of jail. They've worked hard to be where they are. They're the bosses and if Hayden were to go down, he'd lose all the hard work he'd done.

"How many people know that you're taking the fall for Hayden?" I ask, wondering if I'm going to have to keep it a secret.

"Besides Hayden? Only three. You, Finny, and Killian," she tells me with a twisted smile. "If I were to tell Ma or Da, they'd lose their minds and demand Hayden tell the truth. Da's already going crazy at the thought of me going to jail. I'm not telling him, and I've made Hayden swear he'll not say it either."

"How the hell did Killian know?" I ask in reference to our uncle. He's Seamus and Edwina's brother. He's the head of the IRA in New York and was the one who brought Makenna into our lives. He cares a lot about us and is on hand if we need him.

She groans, "He found out I'm on bail and my court date is coming up soon. Then showed up at the house, Ma was happy, and we were all surprised. So, imagine my shock when Killian sits me down and tells me not to go through with lying for Hayden."

My eyes widen. "How did he know?"

She shrugs. "How the hell does he know anything? He told me he was proud of me for wanting to take the blame, but I wouldn't survive a day in prison."

My heart plummets. I've heard the horror stories about what goes on inside prison. It's one thing I've hoped would never happen to any of us and thankfully, we've been lucky and none of the family have been caught, until now.

"I'm going to be fine. Hayden's made sure that he's trained me."

Well at least that's something. Hayden's one of the best fighters there is. He trained Makenna when she moved back to the States. Our Danny is good, but Hayden is even better.

"It'll be fine," she assures me.

I nod, the pain hitting me at full force making me wince.

"Rest, Hol, your body needs it. I'm not leaving. I'll stay with you until either your da or husband comes back."

God, I love my family.

I hope she's right and that she'll be okay. Before I'm able to say anything, the door opens and when I glance at the newcomers I frown, who the hell are they and why are they here? The two men that enter, have cold expressions on their faces. Their focus solely on Jade.

"Who are you?" I demand, trying to sit up and the pain making it impossible to do so.

"I'm Detective Hanna, this is my partner, Detective Nelson." The taller of the men says as he steps forward.

"Okay…" I say, wondering what they're doing here.

The men step forward. "Jade Gallagher you are under arrest for…."

His words fade as I stare at my beautiful cousin, her eyes filled with unshed tears. "I'm so sorry," she mouths to me.

My heart is in my mouth when they reach for the handlebars of her wheelchair.

"Please," I plead with them, my fingers curling into the sheets on my bed as I once again try to sit up. "She's hurt, she should be resting."

"I'm sorry, ma'am, this has to happen." His tone soft, but adamant.

I watch with tears as they take her from my room. God, I want to kill Hayden. My tears fall thick and fast when the door closes behind them. It's too much, today, we've lost too many people and now Jade's been arrested.

The sob that bursts from me is soul wrenching.

I need Romero, I want my husband.

TWENTY-THREE
ROMERO

Stepping into the derelict building the men somehow managed to find, my rage is back with full force. I hear the muffled grunts from Ortega, they grow louder the closer I get to the room he's holed up in.

The sound of flesh hitting flesh fills the house and they're followed by grunts. My gut twists, who the fuck is hitting him? I glance at Denis and see his narrowed eyes and know he's wondering the same motherfucking thing.

Walking into the room where the bastard is being held, I realize it's Danny that's reigning holy hell on Ortega. I can't deny I'm angry but at the same time, I can't deny he deserves to get some punches in just as much as Denis and I do. Holly is his sister, he's the one who held her unconscious body in his arms as he walked her out of that fucking hell hole.

Ortega is standing against a support beam, his feet together, tied around the beam. His hands above his head, also bound to the beam. He has no escape.

"Enough," Denis roars, his body tight as his eyes

promise the hell he's about to unleash. I can imagine what you'd see behind mine.

Danny's body heaves, his knuckles red but the skin isn't broken. Ortega's torso has been worked over. Kidneys, ribs, stomach, liver. Each spot has been meticulously targeted. Danny knows how to get maximum impact from his punches. And damn, I bet Ortega is in some serious fucking pain right now.

Denis takes Danny's place. The Gallagher men are getting their revenge for a whole lot more than just Holly. Denis' brother lies in the hospital and his father is dead, all at the hands of this fucking bastard.

What Denis does, is so unlike his son. Instead of punching him, he whips out his knife, the flick of the switchblade has Jose tensing. He's not stupid, fuck no, he's not, he knows what's about to come and not even fucking God can help him right now.

"You killed my father." His voice is quiet, but like a whip, it makes its impact. "You shot my brother," the smirk on his face is unlike anything I've ever seen. This is a side to Denis very few ever get to witness. Damn. "But your biggest mistake," he says as he steps up so he's face to face with the asshole, "was taking my daughter."

He effortlessly pushes the switchblade into the motherfucker's shoulder, the exact place that Holly was shot. Lightening quick, he withdraws it and rams it into his thigh, again, the same place that Holly was shot.

"Now, I'm going to watch with immense fucking pleasure as you die. I may be a sadistic motherfucker, but he," Denis says pointing at me, "he's your worst nightmare. You are the reason his wife is in hospital, why she was shot. For that he's going to enjoy taking strips from your body." Denis steps back and joins Danny standing against the wall. Every single man is here. Whether they're Irish or Italian, they're either lined up against the four walls or standing somewhere in the house, watching, waiting. Knowing they'll have their revenge.

I smirk, that's not a fucking bad idea. It's something I'm good at, making them cry and pant as their skin comes from their bones. But no, this fucker is going to feel the pain as I break every motherfucking bone in his body.

I walk up to the asshole and crack my neck from side to side. This is going to be fun.

"It was that fucking whore. She never said the ginger bitch was your wife," he spits, the smirk on his face further pissing me off.

Wickedly fast, my fist smashes into his ribs, I hear the crunch beneath my knuckles. Good. It's begun. "That, you fucking piece of shit, is for putting your hands on my wife. You not only shot her, but beat her."

"*Bastardo*," he gasps in Spanish. "I'm going to enjoy killing that bitch, she's pretty for a redhead. I wonder what she'd feel like when I fuck her."

The fucking asshole is baiting me.

Lifting my leg, I bring it down against his shin and listen as he roars in agony. The bone no doubt shattered beyond repair. "You will not fucking touch my wife," I hiss into his face. "She no longer exists for you."

His eyes flash with anger. "Guilty conscience? This is all your fault, you're the reason your wife was taken, why her family were slain."

Guilty? No, I'm not. This isn't my fault, far fucking from it.

"That's where you are wrong. I didn't lead the whore on, she knew the score from the get go." Fuck, I'm not letting this prick get into my head. I've done nothing wrong. I have a past, something I'm grateful Holly doesn't. I can imagine what I'd be like if someone else had her before me. I'd have to kill the fuck.

He snarls at me, "So you'll kill me. What about that bitch?"

I smile. "Don't worry about Georgina, she's being dealt with as we speak."

Melissa and Makenna haven't finished with her ass yet. They have promised to wait until we're back before killing her. I want to watch as that bitch realizes she's going to die, be there when she takes her final breath, and have it so the very last thing she'll see is my motherfucking smile.

I start the methodical torture. Starting with his pinky finger, I break all twenty-seven bones in his hand. Then I move onto the next. Each snap of the bone is music to my ears.

It takes me over an hour to break the majority of his bones. Every bone below his neck is broken, other than his spine. His cheekbones and nose are broken too.

He's in insurmountable pain and I couldn't care less. He deserves this. You don't touch my wife. No fucking way.

My hand cups his nape, this is something I've left until close to the end. When he realizes what I've done, the fear is going to soak in. It's going to claw its way up his body until he's begging for me to end his life. It's the reason I've left his jaw untouched. I want to hear him beg and plead.

I grip his head in my hands and twist with all my might, I hear the snap, and release instantly, his breathing shallow and his eyes wide. I chuckle, "Huh, what are you going to do now, Jose?" I mock him.

"What have you done to me?" It's a harsh whisper, one that's filled with pain and fear.

"You're paralyzed," I tell him with a smirk. "You were

warned, asshole. This was not going to go well for you. Did you truly believe I'd give you an easy death? After what you did?" I scoff. "No fucking way. Now you get to live the rest of your life, paralyzed."

His eyes widen. "No, please."

Ah, there it is, the deep seated fear, the realization of what I have done has sunk in and he's now pleading.

"Please what?" I demand.

"Don't leave me like this."

I blink, is he for real? "What would you have done to my wife had we not found her when we did?"

His lip quivers with fear, as he answers my question without uttering a single word.

"You would have killed her. So, tell me why should I get you help?"

He whimpers, "Please..."

I glance over at Denis and Danny, both of them smiling widely, and Denis nods his head. It's time to end this fucking thing.

"No, you intended on taking her from me. You do not deserve to live." I reach for the bat that Alessio somehow managed to get ahold of and let loose, the bat connects with his head three times before his skull collapses.

He's dead.

Holly's safe.

I breathe easier knowing he'll never harm her again.

One down, one more to go.

WALKING into the room where Makenna and Melissa are with Georgina, I'm surprised to see the bitch still fighting.

Demanding to be let go due to who her family is. She doesn't realize we do not give a fuck.

Today we showed how fucking lethal we can be, and that was only a taste of what we can do. We will gut, maim, kill, and slaughter anyone who stands in our way. Together, the Italians and the Irish stand and reign as one.

Georgina's face is covered in blood, it seeps slowly from her scalp. However the fuck Melissa's managed it, she's not only kept Georgina alive, but also kept the blood loss minimal, or as minimal as it can be. The flap of her scalp is either still intact or balancing against her head. Either way, her skull remains covered. For now, at least.

"Finally," Melissa breathes, a blinding smile on her face as she sees her husband. "Can we end this now?"

My lips twitch. "Have at it. Who am I to stop your fun?"

Makenna's laugh fills the room, "I knew I liked you."

I stand against the wall, Danny to my right and Denis to my left. We gave the girls our promise that they'd get to deal with Georgina, I have no problem with that. I released my blood lust on Ortega. The girls, however, haven't been given the chance to unleash theirs fully yet.

"Now, before we get to the good bit," Melissa begins, her voice loud for the rest of us to hear.

As this is Dante and Makenna's house, only a select few are allowed in to watch. Family, obviously, as well as the right-hand men of the family. The men want to see this bitch die, they want to make sure she's not able to do this shit again.

"Why did your uncle allow this?" She questions and we all wait to see how the fucking bitch reacts.

Dante doesn't believe Carter knew how deranged his

niece is, I on the other hand believe that he must know, he has to see how fucked up she is.

"What?" Georgina gasps. "No, he didn't."

"Then how did you get the Ortega men to do your bidding. I mean, we all know your uncle was trying to build an alliance with them."

Ice burns through me. How did we not know? Of course, Melissa would find that out, she's a hacker, a fucking good one. Seems she's been doing a lot of digging.

"I slept with Jose, it was easy to get him on my side. Blow him a few times, and then he was putty in my hands."

I shake my head in disgust. She's a fucking bitch.

"You had to know once we found out what had happened that there would be war." Makenna snarls, anger radiating from her.

She licks her lips. "No, I thought you'd blame the Russians, especially after killing their man at my uncle's restaurant."

Sneaky fucking cunt.

"It didn't work out for you, did it?" Melissa taunts her. "You've lost everything. The men you had wrapped around your finger, your hair, your looks, and you'll lose your life. But none of them are what hurts the most. It's losing Romero that kills you, isn't it?"

Georgina's eyes flash with anger and hatred as she glares at me. "I would have given you everything," she tells me, and I roll my eyes, damn, she's a fucking broken record. "I loved you and you used me."

Motherfucker. "Right, I'm going to set this straight. I did not fucking use you. I fucked you twice, the rest of the time, you were on your knees with my cock down your throat. That is not love. Hell, I didn't even look at you while you were doing it. You're a spoilt bitch and you deserve everything you're getting."

She screams in frustration and the scream turns to a gargle as Melissa takes the flap to her scalp off and Makenna slits her throat.

The life slowly fades from her eyes and I smile. Good fucking riddance.

"Let's go see Holly," Makenna announces.

"Babe," Dante says with a smirk, "you may want to shower and change first."

She looks down at herself and sees she's covered in blood. "Fuck, don't leave without me."

"Lis, baby, you too," Danny says gently and she gives him a nod before following Makenna out of the room.

"I've got this," Stefan tells us, "I'll have the men clean it up. By the time you're home from visiting with Holly, it'll be cleaned."

Dante gives him a chin lift and we follow him out of the room. "I need a fucking drink," he announces.

"So," Danny begins, once we're in the kitchen, all of us have a glass of whiskey in our hands. "I knew you were fucking crazy, but snapping a man's neck without breaking a sweat and not killing him..." he shakes his head, "Man, that's fucking cold."

I flip him off, the stupid ass.

"In all seriousness, though, where the fuck did you learn that? Paralyzing a man, that takes some skill."

I down the whiskey, loving the burn as it makes its way down my throat. "Dude, you cannot talk. We just watched as your wife scalped someone. Where did she learn that shit?"

He grins. "She Googled it."

I laugh, only in this fucking family is this conversation normal.

"This shit is not over," Dante says as he glances around the room at us, "we'll probably have both the Mexican's and Russians after us now."

Denis and Danny share a look, both of them shrug, not giving a fuck.

"Let them, we'll take them out," I vow, no one will ever have the chance to come after my wife. I'll never allow what happened to her to happen again.

Fuck no.

I'll take them out before they even think about doing it.

WE MANAGE to make it to the hospital without me killing anyone. Dante and Alessio have given Makenna a play by play of what happened with Jose Ortega. Of course, my bloodthirsty sister-in-law was riveted with each word they said and chuckled when she heard how I killed him.

As I step foot into Holly's room, my heart stutters as I take in her tear stained face. "Doll face, what's wrong?" I ask, my feet moving toward her.

"They took her," she cries, "I couldn't do anything, I can't fucking move," she snarls, "I had to watch as they took her."

"Took who?" Makenna demands.

"Jade," she huffs, "the fucking cops arrested her, Kenna."

"Fuck," Makenna clips out and pulls out her cell phone, "Liam, we've got a huge fucking problem..." she begins and walks out of the room.

That's an understatement. There's no way Jade will be able to get away with leaving the state and coming here.

I perch on the edge of her bed. "Don't cry, baby," I whisper as I brush the tears from her face. I wrap my arms around her and pull her close to me. "Your family will sort it out." Even as I say the words, I don't believe them. She killed someone and then absconded.

"Can I go home?" she asks as she rests her head against my shoulder.

My chest burns at her words. I want nothing more than to have her with me where I can protect her. "Let's see what the doctor says."

I press a kiss against her head. A settled feeling washes over me. Those that wanted to cause her harm are dead, she's alive, and she's okay.

I'm going to make sure she stays that way, no one is going to hurt her again.

TWENTY-FOUR
HOLLY

It's been a week since we lost Seamus and Malachy. God, it feels as though it was only yesterday. We're all feeling his loss. My heart hurts for everyone. He was my Granda, and I only got to know him for a little while.

Da, Danny, and Makenna have taken it on themselves to show what happens when you take on the Irish Mafia. In the space of a week, they've bombed the houses of the Ortega gang, the death toll has risen as each day passes. Thirty-seven men, women, and children.

I understand why they're doing it. I get they want their revenge; they want to make the people who took him from us to pay. They want to make them feel the way we do. But it's not something I'd ever condone. Killing thirty-seven people, doesn't replace the men we lost. It'll never bring him back. But I'll never tell them that. My opinion on this doesn't matter. I am not a boss; I am not in the family. I'm just a part of it.

"I'm so sorry Finn," I whisper as I lean forward in the chair and reach for his hand. I gather it in mine and hold it in a firm grip. It's cold and still. As is his body. He's still unconscious, the doctors had to put him into a medically induced coma to help him recover. Seeing him lying here, hooked up to so many machines is heartbreaking.

I feel so much guilt about what's happened. If Ortega wasn't after me, he would never have harmed Finn or had the opportunity to kill Granda and Malachy.

The guilt is intensified as I stare down at my uncle's body. Today, we say goodbye to Granda, and Finn won't be there. He doesn't have the chance to say goodbye to his da. I can't imagine what that would be or feel like. Thinking about how it would be if Da died and I couldn't be there to say my final goodbye makes me want to sob.

"I wish I could make it all better. To take away the pain you're going to feel when you wake up." I squeeze his hand. "You will wake up." He has to; there's no other option. We all need Finn. Not having him around is hard, he's always there with a quick joke and making sure we're all okay.

The door opens and Makenna walks in, she's wearing a black dress and black heels. Much like what I'm wearing, although she doesn't have sunglasses. I'm not as good at hiding my emotions as she is. There's no way I'll be able to get through the funeral without crying.

"I thought I'd find you here," she says softly coming to stand beside me. "You can't blame yourself, Hol, it's not right. You aren't to blame."

I let go of Finn's hand and wrap my arms around my stomach, hoping she'll leave this alone. I don't want to talk about it.

"Do you blame Romero?" she asks and I turn my head to glare at her. She raises her hands in surrender, "Because of him, Georgina started her stupid fucking crusade."

The anger is like a whip, it comes out hard and fast.

I clench my jaw, giving myself a few seconds to breathe

before I say something. "*My husband*," I growl, "did nothing wrong. He had a past. He never led her on and he didn't do anything to warrant her craziness. He is not to blame."

Her eyes widen before a slow smile forms on her face. "I love when you're assertive. You need to let this side of you out more often."

I roll my eyes, only Makenna could swiftly change topics like this. "Seriously, Kenna, I won't have anyone blaming him."

She takes my hand, "I promise you, no one blames him. I was trying to make a point. It's not his fault and it's certainly not yours."

I ignore her comment. I would never blame Rome for what happened. He did everything he could to get me back. That included almost starting a war with the Russian's, thankfully, the Bratva didn't retaliate to the shooting that Romero led. I'm waiting for the call to say something's happened. I pray it doesn't.

"Are you ready?" she asks me.

No, I'm not. Nowhere near ready to say goodbye. But I nod, taking a deep breath as I rise to my feet. My leg throbs with pain, but I've learnt how to breathe through it, it's strapped and in a brace. Romero has been trying to get me into a wheelchair for today and that's not going to happen. I'm not going to my granda's funeral in a wheelchair. I'm standing. Thankfully, the shot I was given by the doctor should tide me over until after the funeral.

I turn toward her, my steps slow and steady as I push past the pain. She gingerly takes my arm and links hers through mine, careful not to jostle me.

"It's going to be okay," she assures me. "We'll get through today, and then we'll make sure this never happens again."

I bite my lip, how I wish that was true. But we're not exactly model citizens, we're part of the criminal underworld.

"Has Killian arrived?" I ask as we move out of the room. Our Uncle Killian was in Ireland when Granda was killed, he was meant to arrive two days ago, but he had other things to take care of.

"Yes, he and Granda Henry are here." Her tone is clipped.

I look at her and realise she's not telling me it all. "What?"

She sighs, "Your ma's here."

Fuck. Just what we need.

"Denis is pissed. He's not spoken to her since she arrived, and Zoe is not happy. She left the kids at home and that's further pissed him off."

I shake my head, not surprised that yet again, Ma's left the kids at home. She usually does it, having children is an imposition to Zoe Gallagher. She never wanted any, but she knew the only way to have the life she lives is to trap my da into getting her pregnant. Da's never made a secret that he doesn't love her, so ma's done whatever the hell she likes as payback.

We reach the elevator and the doors open, my heart soars when I see who's standing there waiting. My husband has his arms crossed over his chest as he leans against the elevator walls. Looking every inch of the badarse he truly is.

"Killian has warned her, she's not to say a word to anyone," Makenna informs me with a smile.

"As long as she steers clear of me, I'll be happy." I don't have the mental capacity to deal with her today.

"Don't worry, doll face," Romero says as he comes to stand beside me, his hand going around my waist and I release Makenna and lean into his body. "Your mother even opens her mouth today, there'll be bloodshed."

Makenna laughs. "The sooner she meets her maker, the better. I know she's your Ma, Hol, but Jesus, that woman has been skirting death for a very long time."

I shrug, it's evil I know, she's my ma and I should love her, but I don't. She burnt her bridges with all her children a long time ago. "Eh, I'm surprised Da hasn't killed her yet." I've always wondered what leverage she has over him. He's never admitted she has, but we all know it's something huge.

Romero's arm tightens around me as he leads me into the elevator. I clutch onto him like he's my lifeline, even though I'm high as a kite from the painkillers the doctor gave me, there's still pain whenever I move. My arm isn't in a sling, thank god, I thought I'd have to be in it, but a week was long enough for me.

"You doing okay?" Rome asks softly as the elevator doors close.

"Yeah, just tired." I've not been able to get much sleep, every time I do fall asleep, I move and severe pain radiates through my body.

He kisses my head, and I can't help but sigh into him. I love this man more than I ever thought possible.

"Any word on Jade?" Dante asks.

"Killian said she took the plea deal," Makenna informs us and my gut churns. God, Jade doesn't deserve this. "She's serving five years."

"That's a good deal, no wonder she took it," Dante replies, a serious look on his face. "It's fucked up she's got to go to prison but there's nothing anyone could have done. As soon as she was brought to the hospital with a gunshot wound, she was in the database and there was no hiding the fact she wasn't in Chicago."

He's right, but it doesn't negate the fact Jade doesn't deserve to be in prison, she didn't commit the crime and yet she's paying dearly for it.

"She's okay, Hol," Makenna assures me. "She's tough, you know she is, hell that girl looks sweet as hell but she's vicious when she needs to be."

I nod. "Yeah, she'll give you a run for your money."

The elevator door opens, and Romero leads me toward the exit. "Doll face, you're fucking pale," he gripes, "the sooner this is over, the better."

"I'm fine," I lie. "I need to say my goodbye, hon, if I don't..." I shake my head, unable to think about it. It's why I hate Finn's not able to say his goodbye.

"I know, that's the only reason I'm letting you go. But as soon as it's over, we're going home."

I love how protective he is, how much he wants to look after me. I've been spoilt in my life by the men I have in it. Da, Danny, Mal, Seamus, Liam, Killian, Hayden, Finn, and Romero. I never thought we'd get to this place, yet here we are, and I feel cherished by my husband.

"Okay," I reply, not going to argue with him.

He helps me into the car, where Neri is our driver. Since the shit went down with Georgina and the Ortega gang, everyone has tightened the security. Neri has been promoted to be Romero's driver and bodyguard so to speak. He's young, probably a few years older than I am but Rome says he's one of the best.

"When we get home, your ass is going to bed." I grin up at him and he shakes his head, "to sleep," he says as he climbs into the backseat beside me. The partition is up so Neri can't hear us.

I pout, "Damn." It's been over a week since we've had any sexual relief and I miss it; I miss the closeness of it.

"Nympho," he quips, and I smile, this is the side to him I love to see. Carefree and relaxed. It's not often this side gets to come out, he's usually tense and on alert.

"You love me..." as soon as the words are out of my mouth, I wish I could take them back. He's made it more than clear to me he'll never feel that way about me and saying those words pierces my heart.

His eyes flash with heat, "Yeah, doll face, I do."

I blink. What the hell? A tinge of a memory comes forth of Romero saying that before, but I can't quite grasp it.

He chuckles. "When you were taken, I realized the truth, well Dante helped me realize the truth. I fucking love you, doll face."

Tears spring to my eyes as my heart melts. I never thought I'd hear those words and now I have, there's nothing better.

"Rome," I whisper, unsure as to what to say.

He gives me his panty dropping grin. "Doll face..."

I wrinkle my nose at him, and he chuckles at me. I rest my head against his shoulder and close my eyes. "I never thought I could be happy while so sad," I tell him, "you make me unbelievably happy, Rome. In the midst of everything that happened, you are what has kept me going."

"Fuck," he whispers, "you can't say that shit to me, not here."

I giggle. "Hon, you're the one who doesn't want sex, not me."

His breath is hot against my ear, "I'm constantly fighting a fucking hard on whenever I'm around you. Every time I see you, I want to fuck you."

"You really have a way with words," I quip. He nips at

my earlobe and need hits my stomach, "Rome, please..." I whine.

The fucker chuckles as he intertwines his fingers with mine. "Later," he promises me.

The car rolls to a stop and I glance out the window and see we're at the church. "I'm holding you to that."

He presses his lips against mine, it's a quick, hard, and passionate one which holds promise of what's to come. Within seconds he's out of the car and opening the door for me.

"Ready, doll face?" he asks as he helps me out of the car.

I nod. I guess, I'll never be ready, but it has to be done. We walk hand in hand into the church, Makenna and Dante a few steps in front of us. My heart fills with pride as I take a look around at the full church, so many people have come to say their goodbyes.

Hudson Brady and his wife Mia are here, Mia gives me a small smile, one I return. The East Street Kings men are here too, they take up an entire pew between them. And everyone seems to be giving them a wide berth. My gaze moves further around the church and I see Romero's cousins, the Conti's sitting down.

So many people have come to pay their respects, it's something Granda would have loved. He was always a people person.

Romero leads us to the pew where Hayes, Hayden, Danny, and Malcolm are sitting. Makenna, Dante, Cian, Patrick, Killian, Edwina, Liam, Da, and Granda Henry are sitting in the row in front of us. Each of their backs straight and stiff. I slide into the pew and sit beside Danny.

Frowning, I lean into him, "Where's Lissa?"

He kisses my head. "Annalise isn't well, and she was up all night getting sick. She caught a bug. Which meant my wife was up all night." He leans forward and shakes Romero's hand. "You doing okay, Hol?"

I nod. "I'm okay, still sore, but that's to be expected."

His lips tighten and his eyes narrow. "It should never have fucking happened," he says low, his voice vibrating with anger. "None of this fucking should have."

"Yeah, I know, but it did, we need to move on from it."

Mal scoffs, "Move on? You were fucking shot and beaten, Holly, we do not fucking get over that."

"They're right, doll face, none of us will ever get over that. This world should have never touched you. It did, and those responsible will pay." Rome's voice is hard. I rest my head against his shoulder trying to soothe him.

"Do you mind?" Ma's voice cuts through the silence and I lift my head to look at her. She's sneering down at Romero. "I want to sit between my sons," she sniffs, as she dabs a tissue at her eye.

"Zoe," Da's voice is quiet but harsh, as he comes to stand beside her. "Take your arse to the back of the church and do it now."

Ma smirks. "I'm so fucking glad I told your little bitch the truth."

Da's eyes narrow into slits, his lips thin. "Repeat that..." he rumbles.

"Shit..." Danny mumbles but makes no movement to get up.

"That whore you've been fucking. She had no idea you were married." The smirk on ma's face is cruel. "You didn't think you could get away with playing me for a fool, now did you?"

Da's hand clamps around ma's arm. "Time for you to leave," he snarls at her. "Go back to the hotel and do not fucking leave." He leans in and whispers something in her ear. Something that has ma paling. "Do not fucking test me, Zoe, you will not win."

Ma huffs and yanks her arm free from Da's hold, "This is not over, Denis," she warns him but thankfully walks away.

God, she's so fucking dramatic.

The funeral mass begins just as Da reclaims his seat. I lean heavily against Rome as the day finally takes its toll on me. I listen to all the things the priest says about Granda and not for the first time, I regret the little time we spent together.

When the choir begins to sing "Amazing Grace", I'm unable to keep the tears at bay.

"Baby," Romero whispers as he kisses my cheek. His arm tightening around me, holding me close to him.

When the funeral mass ends, I see Da's face and the hurt and pain etched in his features isn't just down to his father dying. No, Da's hurting for what Ma's done.

I pray things between him and his woman will be okay, and that he'll be able to fix it. He deserves some happiness in his life. But before that can happen, he'll have to deal with Ma. Otherwise, he'll never be free.

TWENTY-FIVE
ROMERO

Holly shifts beside me, trying to get comfortable. She's still sore, her beautiful face still marred with bruising. They've turned an ugly shade of fucking black and blue, but the swelling has slowly started to recede.

We're still in New York, it's been two days since we buried Seamus, the Irish have finally started to go home. Danny and Melissa left yesterday, neither of them wanting to, but they had too. Denis and Zoe left with Henry this morning. Denis left so he could take his wife with him before I killed her. The cunt kept making comments about my wife and no matter how many times I cut that shit off, she'd continue to do it. So, Denis left, taking the bitch with him.

The front door opens, and I glance at Dante who's currently sitting beside Makenna, both of their expressions blank as they wait for Alessio to enter the room. Dante called him twenty minutes ago, telling him he needed to talk. Of course, whenever the boss calls, you come running, and when the boss tells you he needs to talk, you brace for whatever the fuck's about to go down.

Alessio steps into the room, his face etched in anger. His gaze goes to my wife. "Holly," he growls, and my arm tightens around my wife as my back goes rigid.

"Yes," she replies sweetly as she smiles at him.

"Want to tell me why the fuck my car horn has been changed?" he demands as he takes a seat on the vacant armchair. "The fucking thing sounds like a Dixie horn," he grumbles.

I look down at my wife who's got a confused look on her face. "Wasn't me," she tells him, "Do you think I'd be able to do that while I'm injured?"

Makenna chuckles. "No, but I bet Danny or Malcolm helped you before they left."

Holly smiles but shakes her head. "They would have, if I had asked, but I didn't do that..."

The way she says *that* makes me brace even more. "Doll face, what did you do?"

She grins. "He shouldn't have annoyed me."

Dante rolls his eyes, and I bite back my chuckle. Alessio apologized to her for what went down with the whole Russian and Damini thing.

"I apologized," he tells her.

"She's talking about you sleeping with Georgina," Makenna inputs. "So, what did you do?"

Alessio's phone rings and he tenses, his gaze swinging to Holly. His lips thin. "You are an evil bitch, Holly. This has been going on for the past two fucking days."

Holly merely shrugs, not giving a single fuck.

"What has been?" Dante asks him, "What has she done?"

Alessio throws his phone to our brother, "You answer it," he tells Dante who promptly does.

I watch with a smirk as my brother's body begins to

shake while he talks low on the phone. As soon as the call ends, he bursts out laughing. "How many of those calls have you gotten?"

Alessio sinks back into the chair. "It's not fucking funny, that's like the tenth call today."

"Wait, what am I missing?" Makenna asks, glancing around at us all.

I shrug, I have no idea what my vindictive wife has done.

"I may..." Holly begins, "have posted Alessio's number online. In a sex group."

"What type of sex group?" Makenna asks with a smile.

"BDSM," Dante replies, laughing his ass off. "They want Ales to dominate them."

I close my eyes and bury my head into her hair. Careful not to jostle her. "Baby," I murmur. "The shit you come up with."

"It's not fucking funny," Alessio gripes, "the numbers are unknown. I have to answer my fucking phone."

"Don't piss me off, it's quite simple," Holly tells him. "But I want to find out who did his horn, that was fucking genius."

"Shut up," Ales grumbles, there's no heat in his words. He turns to Dante. "You wanted to talk?"

Dante sighs. "Yeah, we all need to talk."

Alessio sits up straight. His expression shutters. "What do you want to talk about?"

I glare at him; he can't be this fucking stupid.

"I left this talk until now. Holly needed to be here too, and the women needed to grieve for Seamus. You didn't think what went down would go without us properly fucking talking or dishing out a punishment, did you?"

Alessio growls as he leans forward, his hands intertwined. "What do you want to know?" His words clipped.

"Fucking watch your tone," Dante warns, rising to his feet.

"Enough..." Holly says, her words sharp like a whip and we all stop and look at her. Her face etched in pain. "We have lost too fucking much. The last thing we need is friction in the family."

"Hol..." Makenna begins softly, "this is business."

Holly's eyes flash with anger at her aunt's words. "Bullshit, right now, this is family business. You are not his bosses right now, you are his brother and sister, as Rome and I are. It's time to stop with the macho fucking bullshit, it will not work."

"Holly, I get you're trying to help..." Dante's words are filled with respect and warmth. He's grown to love my wife as he has Melissa, they're family.

"I am trying to help. Just fucking listen." She snaps and I blink in surprise, she's never spoken this way to him before. "You're trying to intimidate him into talking. That isn't going to work. Your father," she spits the words out, "used to do the same. Don't treat Alessio like he's a burden or a child, instead, we need to find out why he's done what he's done. We listen to him without interrupting," she says pointedly looking between Dante and me. "When he's finished, then and only then, can we ask questions and dig deeper."

Makenna nods. "She's right. We're not to treat him like a soldier, he's our brother. Right now, this is family business. So, we treat it as we would any other family business."

Dante sighs and takes his seat again. "Okay," he says begrudgingly. "Ales, talk, explain everything from the beginning, let us understand what's happened."

"Thank you," Alessio says to Holly and she rewards him with a smile. "When I was seventeen our father gave me a job to do. I was to infiltrate the Russian Mafia to find out if they were skimming the drugs Dad was running. I was to get as close as I could to them and gain their trust."

Holly twists on the sofa, raising her leg from off the floor and lying it on the couch. She rests against my body, her head against my chest. I close my arms around her and listen to what my brother has to say.

"I got close to Yelena, she's Maksim's granddaughter, the old Pahkan's great-granddaughter and she's one of the Bratva's assassins. I learned a hell of a lot by getting close to her. So much so Dad wanted me to stay undercover for as long as I could." He glances down at his feet, the shame radiating off him. "I should have told you what dad had wanted from me when he died, but that meant I had to admit Yelena was more than a job and I wasn't ready to do that."

I nod, understanding what he meant. Telling everyone he couldn't let her go meant admitting to himself she was more than what he wanted.

"So, I kept her and my task a secret. Never at one stage did I betray the family. I would never do that. Fuck, to have you even think that pisses me off. It's been the three of us against the fucking world since we were kids. Our bond isn't like anyone else's, I would never go against you." The conviction in his voice is enough to make us realize that maybe we were a little hasty in not listening to him.

"I've found out a hell of a lot since I've been in with the Russians. Now Yelena's gone, I won't be able to get that any longer. But I will tell you Maksim is all about peace right now. He's trying to rebuild everything his father ruined and then Dimitri. Going to war with us isn't on his agenda because it's a war he cannot win." Alessio informs us. "Is he pissed, yes, does he want your head, probably, but he doesn't have the manpower, nor the funds to go against you."

Dante sighs. "What you mean is, he'll probably retaliate when we least expect it. When he's rebuilt everything."

Alessio nods. "Yes, but if that ever happens, I have enough information on their operations that we can infiltrate those, take them over, and break them again."

My respect rises for my younger brother. He's obviously done a hell of a lot of thinking about this shit and made some contingency plans.

Dante sighs, resigned to the fact that we're going to have to wait. "Okay, we'll deal with it if it comes to it. What I want to know is, why didn't you tell us you'd be with the Russian's? It's going to take a fucking lot for our men to get over the fact you were at the boxing gym."

Alessio nods immediately. "I know it will. But there was only one reason why I was there. Yelena. I needed to find her, I had hoped her grandfather would lead me into the right direction, but he was pissed I was the reason she fled."

There's utter silence, everyone taking in everything he's said.

"That's it," he announces. "That's what's happened."

Ah, so it's question time.

"Why?" Holly says. "You obviously either deeply care for Yelena or love her. Why the hell did you sleep with Georgina?"

Just hearing that fucking bitch's name has anger coursing through me.

Ales sighs. "It was the biggest mistake of my life. I was a fucking idiot. I tried to pretend Yelena didn't mean that much to me. I'm paying the price for it now."

"Right, I understand all that you've said," Makenna says. "I even understand why you slept with that fucking bitch, but what I don't understand, Alessio, is why you've been acting like a bastard since your father died."

His jaw clenches, this isn't what he wants to talk about. Too motherfucking bad. "Answer her," I demand. Holly's hand reaches for mine and she squeezes it. Christ. Having her in my arms is the best feeling in the world. I'll never get used to her offering me comfort.

Ales sits back in the chair and looks up at the ceiling. "Dad was different with all three of us. He had no qualms in letting the three of us know just how much he hated us. But he tolerated Dante, he was next in line to be Capo. Rome, he gave you a wide berth, I know that was because of whatever the fuck happened when you were younger and had mom going crazy. Both of them were scared of you."

Holly tenses in my arms, her head tilts back so she can look at me, her eyes filled with questions. I knew this day would come, that she'd need answers.

"But with me, he was a fucking bastard. Beaten, starved, you name it. I was his personal fucking punching bag. I had no option but to do as he said. It wasn't until I was old enough to hit back that he finally left me alone. But when he died and everyone started saying how much I was like him and how fucking great the bastard was, I lost it." The defeat in his voice has my gut burning.

"You're not like him," Holly announces. "I've heard the stories of what your father was like. How he'd rape and murder women who went against him. How he'd beat men for even the slightest indiscretion. That's not you, any of you. You may bear his name, hell even look slightly like him. But you are not him."

Alessio shakes his head, not ready to listen to sense.

"Okay, let me put it this way," Holly continues, "do you think your father would give a fuck if he was in the position you were in with Yelena?"

Ales' jaw clenches. "No, he'd have probably killed her."

Holly nods. "Exactly. You are not your father, Ales, you are you. Now it's time to make sure when people think of the Bianchi's they do not see that arsehole. Instead, they see, the three of you and any children that you'll all have. Make the world see you."

My brother glances at us with unbridled fear and excitement. "What about Yelena?"

I look to Dante with a raised brow, wondering if it would be better for him to take the lead on this. But why would we need to when we have Holly and Makenna with us.

"Look, we're not going to sit here and lie. We're not happy you fell for the enemy," Makenna begins.

Holly sighs. "Jesus," she grunts. "What my dear auntie is trying to say is. You hurt her, Ales, in a way I would never forgive Rome if he did that to me. I'm pretty sure Makenna would slice Dante's throat if he did it to her. My advice. Give her space. She ran and that alone tells us she needs the time to heal. Maybe, if she returns you could sort it out, until then, you need to sort your life out. Start living for you. If she does come back, at least you can prove to her you've changed."

Makenna nods in agreement. "This is why Holly's the shit. She's more compassionate than the rest of us. But it doesn't mean she's wrong. If Yelena does come back and sees you've realized what you did was wrong, you may have a chance at fixing things."

"But first," Dante says in his boss tone, "you need to

prove to the men, both Italian and Irish, that you are not a traitor."

Alessio nods. "I will. I'm not stupid, I know I've fucked up, more than I should have. Holly, you of all people should be pissed at me the most."

My wife smiles at him. "Why? You're sorry for what you've done, and you won't do it again." I'm pretty sure there's a threat lingering in her words.

Alessio chuckles. "No I won't. But still, I'm sorry."

"Apology accepted. Now, can we move on from this?" He nods, "Good, can we help in any way for you to rebuild your life? The way you were going, you'd have been dead within five years."

My arms tighten around her again. She's got the fucking softest heart of anyone I know. I'm grateful she's so forgiving and willing to help him.

"Thank you, but right now, I need to do that myself."

Pride fills Dante and Makenna's eyes. I know if anyone looked in mine, they'd see the same reflected in them. It takes a lot for a man to not only admit they were wrong but to restart their life when they've hit rock bottom.

Dante and Alessio talk in hushed tones as I turn to my wife. "Thank you."

She rolls her eyes at me. "This is my family too, Rome, I hate to see it fractured."

I kiss her head. "You ready to go home?"

She nods, a grin slowly forming on her face. "So ready."

My cock starts to thicken. It's been far too long since I've been inside my wife. Tonight, that changes.

TWENTY-SIX

HOLLY

I've been patient, I've waited and waited, hoping he'd come to me when he was ready. But he hasn't and now I want answers.

I draw circles on his chest, we're both naked, finally having given into the urge to be together. It had been over ten days since I had felt that closeness to him and I needed it. He did too, as soon as we kissed, he lost control and I was right there with him for the ride.

"So..." I begin, my finger still drawing circles on his chest. "We need to talk about what Ales said today about your parents and the way they treated you." I keep my voice soft and even.

He sighs, but he doesn't push me away or try to change the subject. "It's not a pretty story, doll face."

My heart breaks already and he hasn't even told me anything. "I guessed that, but I want to know everything."

He rolls over so his arms are around me and I'm tucked up into his chest. "I was eleven. Dante and our father were out, Matteo was grooming him to take over. He'd bring him along to meetings and shit. I was often left home alone and honestly it was the way I preferred it. But this night, our mother was home, she'd just put Alessio to bed and had made her way to her bedroom."

He takes a deep breath, and pressing a kiss against my temple, he continues with his story. "I was downstairs playing video games when I heard voices. I didn't know them and with Matteo gone, most of the men were with him."

My hand stops drawing circles, I press my palm flat against his chest instead as I wait for him to carry on.

"Matteo had insisted I carry a knife with me always. So, this night, I unsheathed it and was ready, I had been taught how to defend myself at a young age. I wasn't scared, I wasn't excited. I was just..." he pauses as if he's trying to find the right word. "Normal. I moved silently through the house, I could hear the men talking, they wanted to get to Mom and Alessio. They knew Matteo and Dante were out of the house."

I tense, kind of knowing what's coming next.

"I killed them. One by one, I slit their throats without a second thought."

My heart breaks for him. He was eleven. No eleven-year-old should have to do that, but it's the way of this life. The younger you are when you kill the more revered you are. It's sadistic and yet, true. "Did you get hurt?" I whisper, as I press a kiss against him.

"No, baby, I wasn't hurt. Mom heard the commotion and came running downstairs and when she saw what had happened, she went crazy, calling me a monster and I was worse than my father." There's no emotion in his voice and I hate it. "She called Matteo telling him about the devil he had created."

I gasp. That fucking bitch.

"Rome," I whisper, unable to keep the pain and anger out of my voice. "I hate that bitch. God, if she were still alive, I'd kill her myself. You are not a monster; you aren't the fucking devil. You're Rome."

His head leans against mine. "Only you see me that way, doll face." His eyes wide as he stares at me in wonder. "I don't know what I did in this life to deserve you, but fuck, I'm one lucky bastard."

I shake my head. "I'm the lucky one."

He closes his eyes as his arms tighten around me. "When Matteo arrived home, he saw the carnage I had wrought. From that day, he looked at me differently. I was no longer the boy he could pretend to ignore, not when his men had also seen what I did. They were warned to keep it under wraps, but they still spoke about it. Matteo could no longer deny I was stronger than him. So, he let me do whatever the hell I wanted."

I swallow past the lump in my throat. "You make me feel safe, loved, and cherished. I don't need anything else in this world. I only want you. You are not a monster; you aren't a devil. You are so much more than what others see you as."

"Doll face..."

"Your family didn't deserve to have you. Your father feared your power. Probably knew he'd have to watch his back, that eventually you'd be the one to kill him."

I know now it was Dante, but the point is still valid.

"Your mom, well, I have no fucking idea what was going through her mind. She didn't deserve to be called a mother."

He chuckles. "I love it when you get all protective."

"You protected your family, Rome. That isn't a bad thing. Fuck, if we have children, I'd be able to rest easy knowing you're their father. That you'd protect them with that kind of love and power."

"When," he replies and I still. "I want children with you, doll face, loads of them. But let's give it a few years first, yeah?"

Tears spring to my eyes. "Yeah, a few years. We can get in loads of practice in making them before that though," I say with a grin.

Rome's hands skim down my body, leaving goosebumps in their wake. "Love you, Holly," he says softly as he lifts my leg and places it over his thigh. His cock at the entrance to my pussy. He thrusts into me and I moan. "So fucking much," he tells me as he begins to move.

This is unlike anything we've done before, it's slow, passionate, and perfect. Our mouths touch and Romero controls the kiss, his tongue sweeping into my mouth, teasing, tasting, and taunting my own. He keeps the slow and languid pace.

My orgasm is building and just like the sex its pace is slow and steady. My toes curl as he continues with the pace. "Rome," I gasp as I feel the pleasure start to wash over me.

"That's it, doll face, I can feel your pussy squeezing my cock." He groans, yet, he doesn't alter his speed. His thrusts are precise and calculated.

"I love you, come for me," I whisper against his lips.

His body tightens against mine and I watch as my handsome husband explodes inside of me.

Once we've both caught our breaths back, he keeps his arms around me. His cock still inside of me. "Sleep, doll face," he tells me.

I don't bother arguing with him, my body is drained of energy. I kiss his lips softly and close my eyes.

For the first time since the shooting, I'm able to find sleep easy.

"MORNING," I hear Makenna say and I whip my gaze to the kitchen door to find my aunt and brother-in-law walking into the room.

"Not that I'm not happy to see you or anything, but what are you doing here?" I say as they take a seat at the kitchen table.

Makenna smiles. "Finn's awake."

My heart bursts with happiness. "He is?" I breathe, relief washing through me.

Makenna nods, her smile still on her face. "He is, he woke up last night and I went to see him. I had to explain everything that happened. Including you being taken and Jade being in prison. He's not happy at all. I thought he was going to rip the fucking cannulas out of his arms and come and find you and check to make sure you're okay before he went in search of Jade."

I lean back against the counter, "That's good, it shows he's still the same Finn."

"Yep, he'll have to do some rehabilitation and shit to help gain the power he once had but I know he'll be okay." The relief is clear to see in her eyes.

Romero walks into the kitchen and does a double take as he sees his brother and Makenna sitting at our kitchen table. "Jesus, I thought you'd have been happy to have some alone time. I know that I fucking was," he gripes as he walks toward me.

I slap his chest. "Finn's awake," I tell him.

"That's good, doll face." He grins at me; he was as worried as the rest of us were.

"Okay, so I spoke to your dad on the way over here and he wants to know if you'll go to Ireland for your birthday in four months' time?" Makenna asks.

"Sure," Romero says, "we'll set it up."

Makenna nods. "Danny and Melissa have already agreed to go if you are, and Mal no doubt will too."

I smile, that will be a good birthday, being surrounded by the people I love the most.

"Can we go and see Finn?" I ask, hoping we can.

Makenna shrugs. "Sure, if that's what you want. I'll let you know he's pissed and looking for revenge."

"How is he going to do that, you've killed everyone that was involved," I say, hoping it's true and they have.

"Yeah, that's why he's pissed," she says with a heavy sigh.

I understand why he feels that way. He's lost so much and he has no one to blame for it.

"Let's have breakfast," Rome says, "then we'll go see Finn." He wraps his arms around me and pulls me close to him.

I rest my head against him and breathe easy. I'm happy, safe, and loved. There's nothing more I want in this world.

HOLLY

FOUR MONTHS LATER

"Did you have a good birthday, baby girl?" Da asks as we exit the car.

I nod, "I did, I'm glad everyone was here." It had been a long time since all of my brothers and sisters were together. But finally, we're all under one roof for the past two days.

The past four months have been pretty uneventful. The Russians and the Ortega gang haven't retaliated, but that doesn't mean security around us has loosened. In fact, Romero's insisted on more for us. He's waiting for the other foot to drop and for a war to start.

Finn is out of hospital and slowly on the road to recovery. He's changed a lot since the day we lost Seamus. He's no longer the man I knew. Who was always there with a quick smile and a stupid joke. Instead, he's withdrawn and distant. Hell, he doesn't want to be around anyone. I can't blame him, but I miss my uncle.

Jade has refused to see anyone since she went to prison. She won't even see Hayden, which has put everyone on edge as no one knows if she's okay or not. Finn has said he'll try to see her, that he'd take the time to fly out and go to the prison, if she agrees to see him just to give everyone a piece of mind.

Romero's arm slides around my waist. "So, what's this event for?" he questions as he helps me up the stairs.

I'm finally healed after what happened, my leg is back to normal, although I do get some twinges now and then, but nothing too bad. My shoulder has recovered well, and I have full range of movement in it. Yet, Romero treats me as though I'm still injured. When I said it to him, he told me he can't get the image of me in the hospital bed out of his mind and it's going to take a while before he can forget I was hurt. So, I let him do whatever he needs to. As long as it eases him, I'm not going to kick up a fuss.

"It's a birthday party for a friend of Mal's..." The way Da sneers friend has Mal shooting him a look.

"Okay, what the hell am I missing?" I ask, glancing at Danny and Lissa and seeing them have the same confused look as I'm no doubt sporting.

"I found out who my biological father is and Da's not happy," Mal tells us. "I understand he's pissed, but I'm not choosing Jerry over him. I'd never do that, as far as I'm concerned, Denis is my father."

I smile, my brother is the fucking best.

"Wait..." Danny says, "Jerry, as in Jerry Houlihan?"

Mal nods, smirking. "Yep, Ma's a fucking bitch."

I glance at my husband who's as confused as I am.

"Jerry Houlihan is the head of the Houlihan gang, baby girl," Da explains. "The shootings and shit around Dublin, that's done by his gang."

Oh fuck. I heard about him, he's flashy and unstable. "Ma has a type, I see," I comment.

Romero's body shakes next to mine, his laughter silent, whereas Melissa giggles loudly.

"Okay, so both your da's are psychos." I shrug. "They should get along like a house on fire, don't you think?" I send Mal a wicked grin, one he returns.

"Yeah, I agree," Danny says. "Da, you're pissed, I get it, but push aside your anger at Jer, he didn't know."

Da sighs. "Fine, I don't have to like it, but whatever."

We're greeted by a beautiful woman who's about Da's age, and she gives Malcolm a fond smile as she shows us to our seats. "You'll finally get to meet your cousin's this evening," she tells him, "Maverick, is happy there's another man in the family. My son is anything but tactile." The smile she has on her face is very telling, she has a lot of affection for Malcolm, which I love. "I'm sorry, I'm being rude. I'm Nicola, I'm Jerry's sister," she walks over to Da and shakes his hand. "I can't begin to understand how difficult this must be for you. But I'm grateful you're here. You're all family now."

She walks away, her smile wide and pure.

"I like her," I say as I glance around the room, it's huge, like a ballroom. "Whose house is this?"

Malcolm shrugs. "Either Patricia's or Nicola's, they're Jerry's sisters who are twins."

It takes a while until the tables are filled, and a few people stopping by to say hello to Da. Romero stays by my side the entire time, like a sentry, he's on guard constantly.

"Fuck," I hear Danny curse and I turn to see Ma strutting in like she owns the fucking place. "Ma, what the hell are you doing here?"

She sniffs as though she's affronted. "Can I not wish my son's father a happy birthday?"

"Take your arse down the table," Mal instructs, he's no longer making polite conversation with her.

Da sighs, knowing she's going to have to sit beside him. "Behave yourself, Zoe, do not fucking piss me off this evening."

Things between the two of them are tense. Da finally told us why he hasn't killed her yet. Ma has evidence against Danny, footage of him killing someone here in Ireland. It was taken years ago, but it's clear to see, from what Da says, it was Danny that killed the man. Ma has hidden the footage and if Da divorces her or anything happens to her, the footage goes to the police. I hate she's doing this, but until we find where it is, there's nothing we can do. She's played a good game. But she'll not win.

"Stop worrying, baby girl," Da whispers as he leans over to me. "Lissa here has found the footage."

Relief washes through me. Thank God.

Lissa smirks. "Yep, her time is finally coming to an end."

The lights in the room brighten as a tall dark-haired man steps up onto the makeshift stage. "I want to thank you all for being here to celebrate with me tonight, it's not every day you turn fifty." He raises his glass and everyone in the room follows suit. "Tonight is extra special," the man's gaze lands on Malcolm and he smiles. Jerry Houlihan is completely different to what I would have imagined. "Not only do I have my sisters here, I also have my nieces and nephew with me. It's been a while since I've had the entire family under one room. Luckily, there's been no bloodshed."

"Yet," a guy yells and his response gathers laughter from the peanut gallery.

"Jessica," he says as he raises his glass and a small, timid girl steps forward with a big smile. "Maverick..." he says and then his gaze goes to the door where a beautiful woman with silver hair and a tight black dress enters, her smile bright, but it doesn't hide the bruising that's marring her face. "Callie," Jerry's voice softens when he says the woman's name.

"Fuck," Da whispers, it's tortured and painful.

The woman's gaze focuses on Da and the smile dies instantly, hurt slashes through her eyes as she takes in Ma sitting beside him.

"Oh, would you look," Ma says loudly. "Your whore's here, Denis."

Callie's eyes narrow in on my ma, she whispers something to the men around her which has them all tensing and looking ready to kill.

"Well," Jerry says as he steps off the stage, "I guess I was wrong about the bloodshed this evening."

"Callie, baby," Nicola says as she goes to stand by the woman, who's no doubt her daughter. "What's wrong?"

But Callie's glaring at my ma, the anger rolling through her is palpable and it makes me shiver.

"Callie-girl," Jerry says as Da gets to his feet, "go on to my office, I'll be along shortly." Callie gives ma one last glare before she turns and storms out of the room.

"It's time to leave," Da announces, "Mal, you can stay, Danny, take your ma home." Danny doesn't hesitate, and he gets up and reaches for our ma. "Holly, it's time for you to leave too."

Romero helps me to my feet, "It's going to be okay, doll face."

Ma has finally learnt to keep her damn mouth shut. She's silently followed Danny out of the house. I glance back at Da as Romero leads me toward the door and see he's moving toward where he last saw Callie.

"What the hell happened?" I ask once we're in the car, Danny and Lissa are with us and Ma's gone. "Where's Ma?"

Danny shrugs. "She fucking vanished. I've messaged Da to let him know."

Lissa grins. "So, Callie. She's real pretty."

I nod, she really is, and she looked so devastated when she saw Ma and Da sitting beside each other. "She's been hurt, you can see the bruising, they've started to fade, but it's still there."

Danny's jaw tightens. "Yeah, someone worked her over."

The rest of the car ride is silent, everyone in deep thought.

ROMERO and I are curled up on one sofa and Danny and Lissa on the other, *The Hangover* is playing on the TV. Neither Ma or Da have come home, and Malcolm has messaged twice telling us shit is going to hit the fan and he'll be home later and let us know. Whatever has happened, I hope Da and Callie can sort it out.

The front door opens, and we all sit up, all our gazes directed to the sitting room. The blood leaves my face when Da walks in.

"What happened?" I breathe as I take in his appearance. His once white shirt now covered in blood, his face is splattered with it along with his pants.

He takes a deep breath, his eyes flashing with unbridled anger. "Zoe's dead."

ARE YOU READY FOR MORE?

Shattered Union is up next:

https://www.books2read.com/ShatteredUnion

ALL THE WAYS YOU CAN FOLLOW BROOKE

Website: https://brookesummersautho.wixsite.com/website

Newsletter: https://brookesummersautho.wixsite.com/website/newsletter

Facebook: https://www.facebook.com/BrookeSummersAuthor/

Join Brooke's Babes: https://www.facebook.com/groups/BrookesBabes/

Bookbub: https://www.bookbub.com/authors/brooke-summers

Instagram: https://www.instagram.com/author_brookesummers/

Twitter: https://twitter.com/Author_BrookeS

ACKNOWLEDGMENTS

To the Hubby and our daughter – Thank you for giving me the time to write. For encouraging me, for being with me every single step of the way. Love you both so very much!

Krissy: As always, you've gone above and beyond for me! There are not enough words in this world to describe just how much you mean to me. Love you muchly. You're the best friend a girl could ever have!

Christine: You are seriously the best! I'd be lost without you! You're one of a kind and I'm so grateful to have you in my life.

Jessica F: Girl, you're unique, amazing, and wonderful. Thank you for being a friend!!

Jessica A: You know how much I adore you, how bloody amazing you are.

Sam: THANK YOU for everything!!

Megan: You are fantabulous! Thank you for always being on hand for anything I need. You're amazing!

And thank you to you, for reading this book.

Brooke xx

Manufactured by Amazon.ca
Bolton, ON